About the Author

Robert Lambert graduated from Oxford in 1973 having completed his History and Education course for the B.Ed degree. Due to his secretarial skills he taught mainly in Further Education until 1998. Since then he has taught abroad, working in Saudi Arabia, Poland, Belgium and Italy. This is his first book.

Robert Lambert

THROUGH THE RAINBOW

AUSTIN MACAULEY PUBLISHERS™

LONDON • CAMBRIDGE • NEW YORK • SHARJAH

A CIP catalogue record for this title is available from the British Library.

ISBN 9781786931313 (Paperback)
ISBN 9781786931320 (E-Book)
www.austinmacauley.com

First Published (2017)
Austin Macauley Publishers Ltd™
25 Canada Square
Canary Wharf
London
E14 5LQ

For Rosemary Lambert

Contents

The Green Door

As Chris and Paul ran down the street, they heard the shop detective shouting for assistance and so they increased their pace, but no one attempted to stop them. Fortunately, the street was virtually deserted. The few pedestrians they met looked a little puzzled as the boys rushed past, but that was all. Eventually, the boys reached a deserted street, where they stopped to rest. There was still no sign of the shabbily dressed man, who they had first spotted in the supermarket. For a few moments, they stood in the middle of the street panting. Chris was the first to recover. He scuffed his shoes against a crack in the pavement.

'So what do we do now?' he wondered.

'We'll have to explain to our parents just what happened at that supermarket.'

'Oh, yes,' growled Chris sarcastically. 'That is a really fantastic idea. And then what? We get arrested for shoplifting.'

'Oh, shut up!' Paul snapped, suddenly tired of the whole discussion. 'What did you expect us to do? I wasn't going to take the blame for that man shoplifting, even if you were. This is a really fine mess to find ourselves in.'

Chris shrugged. 'Yes, and we're the ones stuck with the blame for those missing goods.' His voice sounded tired and somewhat defeated.

'So, what do we do?' Paul wanted to know.

'We'd better get home,' suggested Chris. 'What else can we do?'

'Let's go quietly then, and hope no one sees us,' agreed Paul. 'Wait a moment! We can go down Back Lane, no one will find us there.'

Back Lane was in a remote part of town, seldom used by locals. It was a street really and not a lane at all. On one side of the road, there was a long brick wall, topped with glass and on the other side a row of rather dismal houses. Poor people lived in this part of town and so there weren't many cars parked in the street. As they turned to walk slowly up Back Lane, Chris suddenly grabbed Paul by the arm.

'Look over there!' he hissed.

To Paul's started amazement, there was a crowd of people moving towards them.

'Oh, gosh!' he moaned. 'If they've got a policeman with them, we're done for!'

'Come on!' urged Paul. 'Let's double back the other way.'

'Okay. I just hope you know what you are doing.'

They had hardly started off in the opposite direction when Chris suddenly stopped abruptly, causing Paul to bump into him.

'What now?' he asked crossly.

'Look! There's another crowd!' Chris exclaimed.

'That's impossible. I don't believe it!' Paul hissed. 'Surely they all can't be looking for us? Whatever do you think is going on?'

This second crowd, headed by an immense policeman, was making its way slowly, but purposely towards them.

11

What made things worse was that Back Lane had no side roads running from it. Paul looked about desperately. Then, to his amazement, he suddenly spotted a green door set in the high brick wall. He grabbed Chris by the arm and pointed. 'Let's go through the door. It's our only hope.'

'But it wasn't there a few moments ago,' mused his friend.

'Who cares!' Paul cried. 'Come on! Let's go!'

It was a strange kind of door, painted green, with an odd sort of pattern traced all over it. There were also some words, written in a language that was unfamiliar to the boys. Chris looked doubtfully at Paul. As they hesitated, there came a tremendous cry from the assembled people. To the boys, it was totally mystifying and illogical the way the two crowds had suddenly appeared in Back Lane. To their horror, a great roar arose from the crowd; it was like the baying of hounds when they scent their prey.

'Stop them!' yelled the larger of the two policeman, who had suddenly realised what the boys were about to do. Paul turned the handle of the door.

'Blow! It's locked!' he cried in disappointment.

'Push harder!' screamed Chris.

They both pushed with all their might. To their relief, the door swung open suddenly with a loud groan of protest from its rusted hinges. Gratefully they stumbled inside.

'Shut the door! Lock it! It's our only chance!' Chris commanded.

Bang!

The door clanged shut.

Paul shot the bolts.

Chris turned the key.

'Phew!' gasped Chris. He mopped his brow with a rather grubby handkerchief. 'That was close! I thought the door would never open!'

There followed a sound of clattering feet and a great pounding of fists against the door. One of the policeman shouted angrily at them to open the door.

'Open the door?' queried Chris. 'They must think we're mad.'

The noise grew louder as the two crowds joined forces.

The boys watched with worried looks upon their faces as the door began to vibrate under the weight of the blows it was being subjected to. The door must have been a very strong one, because, despite the beating it was receiving, it showed no sign of collapsing or giving way under the strain of the combined weight of the people outside.

'I only hope that door stands up to the battering they are giving it,' remarked Paul doubtfully.

'Never mind about that now,' Chris replied with a grin. 'We've got away. Let's have a look around, you never know, we might meet someone who can help us out of this mess.'

As Paul and Chris moved away from the door, they looked about them in amazement. The door in the wall had taken them from a wet dirty street into a beautiful garden. Tall flowers stood everywhere, filling the air with a fragrance that was both precious and wonderful. Bees hummed contentedly and birds were flying above the fruit trees. A fountain was playing in the centre of a velvet lawn. There were two stone dolphins spurting water through their mouths into the basin of the fountain, which was in the shape of a crown. Even as the boys looked, a bird flashed like a blue rapier through the silver spray and then soared upwards into the bright sunlight with a sudden flood of golden notes.

'Let's take a look around,' Paul suggested.

'So long as we keep within sound and sight of the fountain, we should be all right,' Chris reasoned.

They began to follow one of the many shaded green walks that led round the garden. There was still no sign of the owner of the garden, so they continued to look about them. The fruit growing on the numerous trees lining the pathways was the most magnificent they had seen. Paul couldn't help thinking it was odd that the birds fluttering around the trees did not attempt to attack the fruit. Bright coloured butterflies floated above their heads, resembling so many painted feathers. They looked as if they were swimming through the sultry air.

Paul wiped his face with his handkerchief. 'How peculiar,' he remarked.

'What do you mean?' Chris inquired.

'Haven't you noticed how much warmer it is here than in the street?'

'Like an everlasting summer,' Chris observed.

'Listen!' Paul urged. A bird trilled a little song from a tree, whilst the bees continued to hum their own counter melody. Yellow pollen dust spilled from the tall flowers standing against the garden wall. Chris decided to take a closer look.

'Gosh!' he gasped. 'Have you ever seen anything like this before?'

Paul hurried over. 'Gold coins!' he exclaimed. 'At least, I think they must be gold. How on earth did they get here?'

Chris shrugged. 'I think they must have grown from these flowers.'

'That sounds crazy!'

'See for yourself.' Chris pointed at the white flowers and as he did so more yellow pollen dust fell.

'I see,' said Paul thoughtfully. 'When those pollen grains reach the ground, they turn to gold. Amazing!'

'Amazing indeed!' muttered Chris.

'You don't sound pleased.'

'I'm not. There is something very wrong with this garden. Very wrong.'

Abruptly, he struck Paul with his hand.

'Leave it alone!' he snapped.

'What's wrong? I was going to take a look.'

'Don't touch anything! Not even the fruit.'

'Can't I take just one apple?' Paul asked crossly. 'I am sure no one will miss it, besides, I'm hungry.'

'Don't touch anything!' Chris warned. 'Whoever heard of a garden quite like this one?' He looked about cautiously.

'This is a case out jumping out of the frying pan and straight into the fire.'

'What exactly do you mean?' Paul asked uncertainly. He had his own doubts over the garden, but was uncertain over how he should express his fears.

'Wet weather outside the garden and then this unseasonably hot weather inside,' Chris said shortly. 'Nothing is natural here.'

Paul thought for a moment. 'If things are that bad, why don't we just pop back through that door?'

'And let that policeman catch us? That is a really brilliant idea, isn't it?' Chris sneered. 'I suppose you are

15

right,' Paul agreed reluctantly. 'But what should we do now?'

'I suppose we could have another look at that fountain, unless you have a better idea?'

Paul shook his head doubtfully.

'What if those people outside break down the door?' he asked.

'We must cross that bridge when we reach it,' Chris said.

'Welcome,' said a voice, which appeared to come out of nowhere.

Chris and Paul swung round in alarm.

'W-who spoke?' stammered Paul.

'I did,' said the voice.

The boys looked all about them, but they still could see no one.

'W-where I-I mean…w-where are you?' Chris stuttered. His voice sounded quivery and his knees had started to tremble.

'Here, where I will always be,' said the voice. The boys looked up and down and the garden, but could see nothing. Chris even tried peering under a large bush to see is he could discover where the voice came from, but the voice just laughed. It wasn't a particularly nice laugh, Chris noted with dismay.

'But we can't see you,' complained Paul.

'And yet, I can see you,' said the voice.

'Where are you?' Chris asked.

'Look this way, carefully,' said the voice.

They both looked towards the fountain.

'I still can't see anything!' Paul hissed.

'Ssh!' Chris hissed back. 'I'm trying to concentrate.'

16

As Paul fell silent, a rainbow appeared over the fountain. Then the same blue bird, which had delighted them when they had first entered the garden, flew low over their heads and passed through the spray of the fountain. The rainbow became more brilliant, until it was so dazzling the boys had to shield their eyes. Then the shape of a man began to appear from out of the mist. He was the tallest man Chris or Paul had ever set eyes upon. A long white beard, tinged with silver, reached almost to his feet. He wore a cloak, which was covered with yellow stars on a black background. Or was it blue? Chris was never sure about this point, because Paul always insisted afterwards that it was blue and not black. Having seen the cloak, Chris had a pretty good idea who the man was. He was some kind of magician or wizard. And yet, Chris thought, there are no such things as wizards.

'Is he from the circus?' Paul whispered.

The wizard, for that is what he was, carefully unwrapped something from his pocket and placed it on his head. It was a tall pointed hat with silver circles on it. 'Ah! That's better,' he said. 'I never feel completely dressed without my hat.'

'Not wishing to be rude,' ventured Paul, 'but why did you take your hat off in the first place?'

'A good question!' responded the wizard. 'Now why did I remove my hat? Ah! I remember! Removing it saves losing it!'

'Losing it?' Chris asked in a puzzled voice.

'Yes,' replied the wizard absently. 'Losing it. You see, my hat blows away when I'm travelling through space, so I have to take it off and put it somewhere safe, or it would

17

disappear and then I would have a hard task finding it again.'

Chris and Paul exchanged glances. The tall man could be joking, but he didn't sound as if he were having a joke with them. He sounded deadly serious.

'W-who are you?' stammered Paul.

The wizard drew himself up to his fullest height (which was very considerable). 'You mean you don't know?' he asked contemptuously.

The boys shook their heads.

'Zardaka,' he said proudly.

'Oh!' chorused the boys. The name, grand as it sounded, meant nothing to them. The magician must have seen the puzzlement that spread over their faces.

'I am the greatest wizard who has ever existed.'

Chris gripped Paul by the arm fearfully.

'I think he's some kind of nutcase! If he is, we'd better make a run for it.'

'No, not yet,' Paul said. 'Things may not be as bad as you think. Perhaps, he is from the circus, especially with such a stupid name as Zardaka. Ask him about the circus.'

'No! You ask him.'

'All right, I will. Are you from the circus?' Paul inquired.

A dangerous light blazed in the wizard's eyes.

'How dare you!' he roared. His voice was so loud it made the earth tremble with its sound. 'How dare you mock one so mighty!' Zardaka raised his finger and pointed it at Paul. The boy felt his legs turn to jelly and then he fell on his face.

'Oh, please don't hurt him!' Chris begged. 'It was my idea to ask you...' He swallowed nervously, as if afraid to continue. Zardaka slowly lowered his finger as Paul raised his head cautiously.

'I-I'm sorry,' he said weakly. 'I didn't mean to be rude.'

'Circus!' stormed Zardaka. 'What do they know of magic? Can they control the seasons, cause the wind to blow from the south instead of the north, or change the direction of the planets?' He snorted angrily. 'Of course they can't! Don't they teach you anything worthwhile at school nowadays, boy?'

Chris shook his head, much too frightened to say anything.

'Please,' said Paul, his voice shaky with fear at what the wizard might do next. 'Please...we...I mean...we don't learn about...I mean...the supernatural.'

To Paul's relief Zardaka nodded indifferently.

'I see,' he said. 'It was too much for you to understand. I should have realised this. In your world you scoff at magic.'

Chris opened his mouth to speak.

'No—don't interrupt. You must begin to understand that things are not the same here in this world as they are in your own.'

Paul raised himself so that he was kneeling on the lawn in front of the fountain.

'Is that how you managed to appear out of the rainbow?' he asked.

'Yes. And, if you remember, when I was invisible, you were puzzled, because although you could hear my voice, you were unable to find out where I was.'

'So, you do have supernatural powers?'

Zardaka laughed, but his eyes did not smile.

'There is nothing stronger than magic here,' he said softly.

This piece of information sounded more like a threat than an explanation.

'But you must tell me something about yourselves,' Zardaka insisted. 'I have talked long enough about myself.

Paul and Chris exchanged glances, wondering what they could say. Zardaka smiled at their indecision. 'Excuse me,' he said. 'I must take a sip from this fountain. The water is quite exquisite.'

'We didn't mean to come here,' Chris said.

'No one ever does,' Zardaka said. 'However, once I make up my mind to bring them here, they cannot choose to do otherwise.

Paul felt that this sounded rather ominous, but he did not like to say anything that might upset the wizard.

'What Chris meant to say,' began Paul, but the wizard interrupted him with a wave of his hand. There was a dangerous light glittering in his eyes, which made the boys shrink back from him in alarm.

'Have you tried the water?' he asked.

'No—nor the fruit,' Paul replied hastily.

'I'm glad you didn't touch the fruit,' said Zardaka. The dangerous light in his eyes faded. Paul shivered slightly. He felt very glad that he hadn't eaten any fruit, or kept the gold coins, even though both he and Chris had been tempted.

'It is forbidden fruit, at least, to those who are not wizards. Only those connected with magic can taste their sweet juices. I don't suppose that either of you are connected with magic?' Zardaka asked abruptly.

20

'Indeed no!' stammered Paul, not expecting the question. That was the wizard all over. One minute he was all smooth and smiling and the next, hard as flint, dangerous as a rattlesnake, glaring at them with cold, cruel eyes.

'That is strange,' muttered the wizard. He sounded as if he were talking to himself, rather than to Chris and Paul. 'I certainly felt magic in the air when I landed from that rainbow, and it was not my magic that I felt.'

Both boys felt rather uncomfortable as Zardaka stared at them for a few moments, before allowing a wintry smile to break out across his face.

'The water is capital, try it,' he offered.

Paul hesitated. To refuse might mean running the risk of offending the wizard, and that would never do. Chris, however, didn't hesitate for a moment. Boldly, he stepped forward and drank deeply at the fountain.

'Well done!' Zardaka congratulated Chris. 'At least you have courage. I am pleased with you, because you have the kind of spirit which I admire. Now, what about your friend?'

'Go on,' urged Chris. 'Try it.'

Gingerly, Paul drank. The water was sweet and powerful, not like ordinary water at all. It was astonishing how the water took away all his hunger and thirst immediately.

'Excellent!' Zardaka laughed and then clapped his hands. A large blackbird landed on his shoulder. He spoke to it in a strange language and it flew away. He noted the look of curiosity on Chris's face.

'One of my many servants,' he said by way of explanation. 'And now, you must come and look at the garden properly. I believe we all have some unfinished business to attend to.'

21

Chris and Paul followed the wizard through his garden. From time to time he would stop, sniff a flower, tell them something about it and then pass on to another, or he would point out a gloriously coloured bird, urging them to pause and listen to its beautiful song. Even the bees were not frightened when disturbed from their work; they would rest on Zardaka's fingers without stinging him, before flying on to another flower.

'How is that your garden stretches for such a long way?' Chris asked.

'We appear to have walked miles, but we still don't appear to have reached the other side of your garden.'

'Yes,' agreed Paul. 'When we were walking down Back Lane, the wall outside didn't appear to stretch that far.'

'So, my garden appears small from the town?'

'Normal size, perhaps,' Chris admitted.

'Excellent! Excellent!' smiled the wizard and he rubbed his long bony fingers together.

The boys looked at each other with puzzlement written plainly on their faces.

Paul mouthed the word "magic" at his friend and Chris nodded. Magic must be the reason the garden appeared to be much larger than it really was.

There was so much to see and Zardaka took his time making the boys' acquainted with his domain. He walked slowly, talking, stroking his magnificent long beard. Bright multicoloured butterflies hovered over his head wherever he walked and multicoloured exotic birds sang sweet songs as they passed.

'Do you hear something?' the wizard suddenly asked.

'Only the birds,' said Paul.

22

'I didn't mean that. Listen!'

Zardaka broke the stem of a flower between his fingers and the birds around him fell instantly silent. Very far away, like a whisper or a sigh, an almost inaudible shout reached their ears. Both boys knew immediately what the sound meant. The crowd and the police, had not abandoned their search.

'So—they are still after us,' murmured Paul.

'We'll soon see about that!' said Zardaka grimly. 'Follow me!'

After a few minutes' walk, they reached the fountain. A loud banging reached their ears and they could hear the cries of angry people.

'Hey!' shouted a loud ugly voice.

All three looked in the direction of the shout. One of the policemen had succeeded in getting himself a ladder. He was now trying to negotiate the broken glass set in cement at the top of the brick wall, which divided the street from the wizard's garden. Chris and Paul were rather frightened when they saw the angry policeman, but Zardaka didn't appear concerned. 'Hey!' shouted the policeman. 'I want you!'

'Do you mean me, sir?' inquired the wizard in an ominous tone. The crowd outside the green door fell silent at the sound of the magician's voice. They sensed that the drama was about to begin. A few people had hoisted themselves on to the wall, despite the hazard they faced from the broken glass, but they stopped moving when they saw Zardaka. Indeed, he was a fearful sight, nearly seven feet tall, with a beard that must have been over five feet in length.

'I asked you, do you mean me, sir?' repeated the wizard.

'No! Not you! The two boys!' shouted the policeman fiercely. 'I've got a warrant for their arrest.'

'On what charge?' inquired Zardaka.

'Shoplifting!' was the reply.

'Indeed!' said Zardaka. If the policeman hadn't been so angry himself, he would have got down from the wall there and then, before any real trouble started, but he didn't.

'I want those two,' he said obstinately. 'The curly haired boy and the dark haired lout.'

'Oh, I say!' protested the boys.

'Hold your tongues!' snapped the wizard. 'I'll deal with this!'

'That's right,' said the policeman. 'Don't stand any nonsense from them. Now, if you'll just open your door, proper like, we can soon get those two out of your way. Can't say fairer than that, can I?'

'Is it true that you are accused of shoplifting?' asked Zardaka.

'Yes but we aren't guilty. It is all a terrible mistake,' said Chris.

'The boys say it is all a terrible mistake,' Zardaka told the policeman. 'I believe them and think you should give up your search.'

'But I have a warrant for their arrest,' protested the policeman.

'I want to see that warrant first,' Zardaka said.

The policeman threw his warrant at the feet of the wizard. Zardaka snapped his fingers, and a blackbird flew across the garden, picked the warrant up and placed it into

24

the wizard's hand. Zardaka glanced at it and then tore it to pieces.

'This is what I think of your warrant,' he said contemptuously.

'You'll be sorry for that!' shouted the policeman. The crowd roared its approval.

'I can easily get a new warrant.'

'Get off my wall this instant!' demanded the wizard.

A few of the less brave men jumped off Zardaka's wall, but the policeman stood his ground and ignored the wizard's demand.

'The two boys had better come with me, or else!' shouted the policeman.

'Or else what?' asked the wizard in an icy voice.

'They'll be locked up for a very long time and you with them if you're not careful. Aiding and abetting criminals is a very serious charge, I might tell you.'

'And you are trespassing by sitting on my wall,' shouted the wizard.

'That may be,' said the policeman ponderously. 'But let me remind you, you have no right to obstruct an officer in the course of his duty.'

'You have no authority over wizards!' snapped Zardaka.

Light dawned on the policeman's face. He looked down at the other officer waiting down in the street and they exchanged sniggering glances.

'A wizard, eh?' he said reaching for his notebook. Who did this strange looking man think he was kidding? Bah! These crooked people got more stupid with their stories every day. As if he didn't have enough to do, what with petty pilfering and youths driving cars without the owners' permission. 'So you are a wizard?' he said, licking his pencil, so that it would write properly.

'That is correct,' replied the wizard, drawing himself up to his full height. There were a few rude laughs from the crowd. Taking his cue from the people behind him, the policeman decided to have a little fun at the wizard's expense.

'Then you must be from the circus,' said the policeman.

'How dare you!' screeched the wizard turning purple with rage. 'Fortune tellers! Circuses! Those people are amateurs! Pure amateurs! Dabblers! Do not insult me! I have the honour, sir, to be one of the seven who sit at the Grand Oval.'

'Oval?' said the policeman in a puzzled tone. 'You like cricket then? I didn't know you circus folk went in for that sort of thing. Know I do—play a bit when I can. Course, I have to watch my weight.' He patted his stomach reflectively and the crowd roared with laughter. 'What position do you play? Are you a bowler or batsman?'

Zardaka looked as if he were about to burst with rage. Chris and Paul felt really frightened by now. Zardaka's rage was truly terrifying and both boys guessed it wouldn't take much to send him over the top. Unfortunately, the policeman didn't appear to notice that he was in any sort of danger.

'Grand Oval member I shall have to write this all down,' he said calmly.

'You will get down from my wall!' stormed the wizard.

'Oh? So it is ordering the police force you're about now,' said the policeman truculently. 'Well, let me tell you something, Mister-Whatever-Your-Name-Is.'

'Zardaka,' said the wizard.

'Mister Zardaka—that's right!' said the policeman sarcastically. 'Now, as I see it, you have two choices. Either you can give up those two rascals to me, or would you prefer me to get these good people outside to knock down your door for you? It can easily be arranged. The choice is yours.'

'Get down from my wall!' shouted Zardaka. 'Get down this instant! I will not be spoken to, as you have spoken to me.'

'Now! Now! If you are going to take that tone of voice with me,' said the policeman. 'I shall have to come over this wall to arrest you as well.

The wizard began to mutter in a strange language.

'And don't start swearing at me!' warned the policeman. 'That will only make the situation worse.'

'Oh heavens!' Paul groaned. 'Something terrible is about to happen!'

'I will give you one final chance,' said the policeman. 'Give up those boys and I will press no charges against you. Resist me and we will have to smash your door down.'

'No!' thundered the wizard. 'I will not open the door for you, or anyone else. This is my garden and I do as I please here. These two, whatever they may have done in your world, have offended no law in my world.

'He said "world",' said Paul, looking at his friend with frightened eyes. Chris did not answer. Events were beginning to move much too fast for him. He felt stunned by everything that was happening, and could not trust himself to answer.

'Very convincing!' sneered the policeman. 'Right then! Don't say you weren't warned.' He turned to give his order to the people waiting below, but the order was never given, because something awful happened. Zardaka muttered some horrible words, pointed at the policeman with his left hand. A long blue streamer of flame shot like a lightning bolt from the wizard's fingers. The flame touched the constable on the shoulder. There was a puff of silvery smoke and the policeman disappeared! All that was left of him was his helmet lying on the top of the wall and a small green snake. The snake soon came slithering and hissing angrily down the wall. It fell awkwardly into some bushes growing by the garden wall and slipped out of sight.

'As for the rest of you stupid fools,' snarled the wizard, raising his hand and pointing it at the sky, 'have a taste of this!'

"This" was a great thunderbolt which shot across the town at a terrific speed, before exploding with a terrific noise. Then great drops of heavy rain fell over the town, but mysteriously not one spot touched the wizard's garden. There was another flash and explosion and then the people on the other side of the wall began to shout, before running off screaming in all directions. Then all was quiet, except for the steady hiss of falling rain outside the garden. Zardaka stood there smiling a peculiar smile.

'That should settle them. You should have no more problems,' he told the boys.

'But what have you done this to them?' Chris asked anxiously.

'You haven't hurt them, I hope?' inquired Paul.

'No—of course I haven't. I merely frightened them a little. I should think my little exhibition will teach them to steer clear of my garden for a while.'

'Did your magic turn the policeman into a snake?' Paul asked.

'Of course. Rather clever of me, wasn't it? Unfortunately, it is not a spell that lasts long, but one which serves its purpose. Next time, presuming there is a next time, he may not be so lucky.'

'That was rather cruel,' Chris ventured to say.

'Was it?' the wizard laughed. 'I thought it was rather amusing.' Chris and Paul could think of nothing to say in reply to this. Zardaka seeing their indecision, ordered them to follow him.

This time the wizard led them in a different direction through his garden. He walked so fast they had difficulty in keeping up with him. Eventually, they reached the wizard's house. It was a very old house, made of greystone, with red creeper clinging to the ancient walls. Funny pointed windows winked at them as they made their way past the two stone dogs guarding the entrance. The wizard led them up the steps, through the heavy oak door and into the entrance hall. The marble floor was smooth and cool to their feet and the tall pointed windows threw strange patterns everywhere; it was as if the sun was bewitched once it had entered Zardaka's house. A faint musical sound made Chris look upwards. Tinkling chandeliers threw glittering patterns of star shaped light into his eyes. Together they gazed at the rare rugs, the rich tapestries, the strange Eastern furniture which filled the wizard's house.

Zardaka brought them to a room with tall windows which reached the ground. The room overlooked a part of the garden. A table had been laid for them with all sorts of things to eat. There was white and brown bread, strawberries, honey, cream, cakes with thick white icing, jellies, ice-cream and cups filled with curious frothy liquid to drink. The wizard told them to make themselves at home. They were to call him when they had finished by ringing a tiny silver bell which stood on a side-table.

For a few seconds the boys stared in wonderment at the table. The windows were open to the garden and bright coloured butterflies hovered between the garden and the room. Paul was the first to make up his mind. He moved towards the table.

'Supposing it's poisoned?' suggested Chris in alarm as Paul crammed a large portion of sugared cake into his mouth.

Paul made an inaudible remark.

'Manners!' exclaimed Chris in disgust. Paul took no notice.

'My mother,' said Chris in a prissy voice, 'always insists I start upon the bread and butter first and then go on to the cakes and things.'

'Sorry,' apologised Paul. 'You wouldn't let me eat any of that nice fruit growing in the garden and now I'm making up for lost time. In any case, I could never get used to all those stupid rules and regulations about eating bread and jam first.'

'A fine excuse!' snorted Chris.

Dubiously he looked at the food. After a long pause, he picked up a piece of bread and butter. He tasted it gingerly and then began to eat it piece by piece.

'It is good!' he declared.

After they had eaten their meal, the boys sat and talked over all the recent events. Both of them were worried about getting home and wondering what their parents would say when they arrived home. Maybe there would be a couple of policemen waiting for them? How on earth were they going to explain about the shoplifting at the supermarket? Before they had finished their discussion, Zardaka arrived. 'I'm glad you enjoyed your meal,' he said. 'And now, I expect you would like me to show you to your rooms. After all, it has been a long and tiring day.'

'Thank you,' said Chris, 'but I think we should be going home now.'

'I'm afraid that isn't possible,' said Zardaka. 'In any case, it will soon be dark. Why not wait until tomorrow? Tomorrow we can have another little talk and I will see if I can find a way out of the situation you seem to have gotten yourselves into.'

'Thank you very much,' Paul said politely. 'That would be most helpful.'

Zardaka led them up a sweeping staircase, where ghostly flickering's, made by strange shadows, flitted over their heads. Chris and Paul could hear a mysterious whispering all around them as they climbed the stairs. They were a little alarmed by these sounds at first, but as the wizard took no notice, only pausing from time to time, urging them to hurry, they decided the whisperings were harmless. Besides the ghostly sounds and the flickering lights, there was a strange kind of electricity in the air, which sent weird tingling up and down their spines, making them uneasy with the force of these strange sensations. At last they reached a long corridor. Like the garden, the house appeared to stretched forever. Paul tried to remember how many doors they had passed, but there were so many that in the end he lost count. Every door looked the same and none were numbered.

Finally Zardaka stopped. 'Here is your room,' he said to Chris. 'And this is your room, next door,' he told Paul.

They thanked him.

'You will find everything you need inside. If there is anything else you require, you will please ring for assistance. My servants have orders to bring you to my quarters, sometime tomorrow.'

'But…' Paul began.

The wizard raised his hand.

'I would not advise wandering about on your own in my house. Goodnight!'

With this abrupt farewell, Zardaka strode off down the corridor, his long cloak billowing out behind him like some fearful shadow.

Chris and Paul wished each other a doleful "goodnight" before making their way into their allotted rooms, each wondering whether they had done the right thing by going through the green door. Perhaps it might have been better if the policeman had caught them? Only time would tell.

In the House of Zardaka

Chris slowly opened his eyes and looked round the room, bewilderment spreading over his face. He had expected to find himself in his own familiar narrow bed with his mother shouting up the stairs to tell him that breakfast was ready. That was the way he usually woke up, but this room was quite different from the one he knew. Then suddenly he realised where he was. He drew back the curtains and the sun came streaming into the room. Chris looked through the window, but there wasn't very much to see and he was disappointed. All he could see was a forest of fir trees. Then Chris rubbed his eyes in disbelief. This was ridiculous! he thought. How was it possible to own a house in the middle of a garden and yet, at the same time, have a pine forest overlooking it. No, there was something wrong somewhere. Perhaps it was another of Zardaka's tricks. He heard a knock at the door. Chris opened the door cautiously; he was a little nervous of what he might find outside.

'Oh, it's you,' he said to Paul. 'I was wondering when you were going to show up. We've got quite a few things to discuss.' Then he looked at the clothes Paul was wearing. 'How did you get those clothes?' he demanded.

Paul shrugged. 'They were hanging up in the wardrobe, so I thought I might as well wear them. Do you think they suit me?'

'You look ridiculous!' Chris snapped. In fact, they were fantastic clothes, made in fine velvet, the kind of thing a prince might wear, but Chris wasn't going to let Paul know that!

'There are some clothes for you, just like mine, hanging inside your wardrobe,' said Paul. 'Why don't you put them on?'

'All right, I will,' Chris declared. 'Have a look through my window whilst I get ready to meet Zardaka.'

'Good heavens!' Paul shrieked.

'What is it?' Chris asked innocently.

'There is a pine forest outside your window,' gasped Paul.

Chris shrugged. 'What of it? You are on the same side of the house, so you probably have the same view. Didn't you notice it?'

'Of course I did. Looking through the window was the first thing I did. I have a different view to you!'

'What!' Chris exclaimed. It was his turn to be startled. He began to dress as quickly as he could. 'Come on!' he urged, when he was ready. 'Let's have a look through your window.'

'I don't believe it!' Chris cried. He rubbed his eyes in disbelief, but the view remained the same. Despite Paul's warning he hadn't been prepared for anything like this. He found himself looking down a sheer cliff. At the bottom of the cliff was a raging sea, lashed by angry clouds, scudding across a lead coloured sky.

'Perhaps it is some kind of joke,' suggested Chris when he had recovered from the shock of looking through Paul's window.

'This is no joke,' Paul scowled. 'Watch what happens when I open the window.'

As he opened the window, a terrific gust of cold air filled the room, nearly tearing down the curtains. Heavy drops of rain splashed into their faces and there was the distinct tang of brine to prove that it was real sea air spilling into the room. It took the combined efforts of Chris and Paul to close the window.

'Well? What do you make of that?' demanded Paul.

'You'll have to ask room service for a change of view.'

'This is no laughing matter!' stormed Paul. 'I could have been blown away quite easily in the night, quite easily!'

'If it is a joke, then it's pretty sick,' Chris agreed. 'Maybe it is just Zardaka's way of making sure we don't escape in the night.'

'I wonder if every room in the house has a different view,' Paul mused.

'What good would that do us?'

'We could escape.'

'How? By crawling through the pine forest?'

'Why not?' asked Paul.

'Have you ever tried crawling through trees?' Chris asked.

Paul shook his head.

'Then you don't know what you're talking about!' cried Chris.

'We could at least try,' Paul persisted.

Chris thought about it. 'We would have to be very careful how we did escape,' he said. 'You saw what Zardaka did to that fat policeman?'

Paul frowned. 'Has he really got all that power, or was it some kind of trickery?'

'I would have thought that the view from this window proves Zardaka is what he says he is,' Chris said carefully.

Paul opened his eyes wide. 'What? You believe all that mumbo-jumbo? That this is his world, so we are bound by his rules?'

Chris nodded.

'I don't like the sound of that at all,' Paul declared. 'I can't help thinking it might have been better if that fat policeman had caught us.'

Chris shook his head doubtfully.

'If we just follow the rules and don't try to understand them, we might find a way of outwitting Zardaka. Surely that would be better than trusting our luck with that fat policeman?'

Paul sighed heavily. 'I suppose you are right. Only, it seems to me, just as things starts to make sense, something else comes along and turns everything upside down again.'

'Why don't we have a look around?' Chris suggested.

'What about Zardaka?'

'We'll be very careful. All the doors in this corridor look the same, so we'll leave your door open. At least that way, we'll know which room to come back to.'

'We could use this chair as a wedge,' Paul suggested. Chris nodded approvingly. 'That should do the trick— unless someone comes along and tampers with it,' he added darkly.

The first room they tried looked uninteresting. It contained similar furnishings to the rooms that Chris and Paul had spent the night in. Chris was about to close the door, when he spotted something unusual. The view from the window was different. A snowy plain stretched away from them into the shadowy distance. Paul cautiously opened the window and then hurriedly slammed it shut. It was bitterly cold outside.

'Hm!' commented Chris. 'Not particularly inspiring, is it?' The next room overlooked a hot inhospitable desert with white bones littered about. There wasn't a single tree to be seen. Paul didn't both to open the window, one glance at the blood red sun hanging in the yellow sky above that desert was enough to convince him that this was no illusion. The third room revealed a hot sweaty jungle, through which no traveller could possibly force a passage. Alligators lurked in the brown waters, and snakes crawled everywhere, whilst decaying vegetation supported new plants as they struggled for the sun.

'Don't open the window!' Chris warned.

'Why not?'

'The insects in that jungle would torment us. Besides, there must be fever in that rotting marsh.'

An endless cavern greeted their eyes in the adjoining room, filled with red flames and billowing sulphurous smoke.

'Not much hope there either,' muttered Paul.

The next view was even more terrifying. Both boys shrank back from the awesome sight. An enormous volcano blotted out the sky, and molten lava came tearing down its steep sides towards them.

Chris shut the door hurriedly with a loud bang.

'I think I am beginning to get the idea at last,' he said.

'Would that volcano have harmed us?' Paul asked.

'I don't know,' Chris confessed thoughtfully. 'One thing I do know—I'm certainly not going to risk my life trying to find out.'

'But we don't give up trying to escape?'

'We certainly don't,' Chris declared in a determined voice.

They made their way back to the room they had started from. The chair, much to their relief, was still in place.

'Let's call for breakfast,' Paul suggested.

'How do we call for breakfast?' Chris asked.

'I think Zardaka just clapped his hands.'

Chris obediently clapped his hands.

Two shrouded figures instantly appeared.

'Your wish is our command,' said one in a deep voice.

'We would like to wash and then to have breakfast,' said Chris. The figures motioned that the boys were to follow them.

When they had finished breakfast, the two figures glided back into the room, cleared the table and noiselessly disappeared.

'Let's go into the garden for a bit,' suggested Chris. 'It is much too nice a day to stay inside.'

'I thought we were going to explore?' said Paul.

Chris put a warning finger to his mouth. Paul guessed that his friend suspected that there were spies in the house who would report anything that was said by the two boys to Zardaka. Once outside, they wandered aimlessly, exploring the pretty little grassy walks which ringed Zardaka's house. Neither of the boys dared discuss their plans for escape, until they were quite satisfied they would not be overheard. Suddenly, Chris clutched Paul's arm.

'Hush!' he hissed. 'What was that? I thought I heard something. Did you?'

'Yes—it came from over there. Quick! We'd better hide behind those bushes.'

'That doesn't sound like Zardaka,' said Paul. 'Who on earth could that be?'

'Better keep down for a bit,' Chris advised.

The footsteps came nearer. Chris and Paul huddled closer together in the middle of the bush. Then the footsteps stopped. Chris cautiously looked out. Then he gasped, almost choking with surprise. Paul pushed him aside so that he could have a look for himself.

'Goodness!' exclaimed Paul. 'It's the fat policeman!'

'The spell must have worn off,' said Chris. 'What are we going to do?'

'Why not make friends with him,' sniggered Paul. 'And then we could ask him to arrest the wizard for us.'

'Hey! That's not such a bad idea!' Chris said approvingly.

'What?' hissed Paul. 'Are you off your rocker? Look! I was only joking. Don't you see. He's after both of us, but if it hadn't been for us seeing the green door, we would have been captured by now.'

'Things have changed since then.'

'Oh yeah? Your opinion is your opinion. Only, I wouldn't trust that policeman any further than I could throw him.'

'I'd like to see you throw him.'

'This is no laughing matter!'

'I know it isn't.'

'Then stop joking about it!'

'All the same,' mused Chris thoughtfully. 'We ought to do something. That policeman might be our only chance of getting out of here and away from Zardaka. We can't stay here forever you know.'

'You could be right,' Paul agreed. 'If we could get that policeman on our side, we might just be able to convince him of our innocence over that shoplifting charge.'

'Just one thing,' cautioned Chris. 'We ought to wait a bit, maybe follow him, find out what he is up to, before we make a move to speak to him.'

Very carefully the boys followed the policeman. Eventually, they reached the fountain where they had first met Zardaka. To their surprise, the policeman appeared to be very interested in the fountain. If he no longer had his helmet, he still had his notebook. The boys heard him mutter several times to himself as he began to write quickly, the blunt pencil scouring the page with strange squeaking sounds. Then the policeman abruptly stopped writing and scratched his head.

'He doesn't appear to be too pleased with the way things have been going,' noted Paul.

'Nor would you, if you had been turned into a snake.'

'Do we speak to him now?' Paul wondered.

Chris hesitated. Now the moment had arrived, he no longer felt confident over speaking to the fat constable. As he looked, the policeman, who appeared to have completed his investigations of the fountain, was now examining the garden wall. The wall presented a daunting spectacle, with its row of broken glass set in cement, several metres above his head.

'Impossible!' muttered the constable, wiping his hot face with a spotted handkerchief. 'There must be a door somewhere.'

'Perhaps this is the time to identify ourselves,' suggested Paul.

Chris nodded his approval.

Slowly, they emerged from their hiding place. The policeman had reached the point in the wall where his helmet was still perched on top of the wall. He stood looking at it with a perplexed look upon his face.

'Now, how on earth did that get there?' he wondered.

'Excuse me,' said Chris.

The policeman spun round. It was quite comical, as his jaw hung open and his eyes were bulging and his fingers had started to stray for the police whistle.

'Oh, please don't!' Paul begged. 'You see, the wizard might hear you.'

'But...' began the fat policeman.

'Hush! Not so loud!' Chris warned. He put his finger to his lip.

'We are not safe here. Zardaka's spies are everywhere. Don't make a sound. We are both quite willing to go with you, when the time comes, but there are several things you should know before we can do that.'

'And I have quite a few questions to ask you myself,' said the policeman sternly.

'Oh dear!' gasped Paul in horror. 'You aren't still after us?'

'Duty is duty—as they say!' said the policeman grimly, fixing him with a fierce eye.

'All right,' said Chris wearily. 'Ask away, but just don't make too much noise.'

41

'All right; I'll agree to that, but no tricks.'

The policeman followed the boys, who made straight for a tangle of bushes, not far from the fountain. 'Now then,' he said. 'Tell me the truth.'

'First,' Chris began, 'we don't bear you any grudge. Is that understood?'

'Quite,' said the policeman. 'I'm Higgotty. What are your names?'

'I'm Chris and he's Paul. We had to escape, because we felt, quite rightly in our view, that we'd broken no laws. At least, we hadn't done anything which caused harm to anyone.'

'That is beside the point,' said Higgotty. 'People don't run away; at least, not unless they have something to hide.'

'I'm coming to that,' interrupted Chris. If you'd only let me finish…'

'And I had a warrant,' pointed out the policeman.

'Not to begin with,' said Paul.

'That is true.'

'So why did you come after us with all those people?' asked Paul. 'One minute Back Lane was deserted and the next there were two crowds of people coming after us.'

PC Higgotty scratched his head.

'That was quite puzzling as to how all those people suddenly turned up. All I know is that we received a tip from an unidentified caller.'

'How convenient!' sneered Paul. 'What exactly did your informant tell you?'

'The caller told us that two boys had just carried out an unsuccessful raid on a supermarket. We were also informed at police headquarters where you could be picked up.'

'Do you mean in Back Lane?'

The constable nodded.

Chris exchanged a meaningful glance with Paul.

'How did you know we were the boys?' Paul asked curiously.

'The description the caller gave matched the one given to us by the store detective.'

'Before you continue, you must believe me when I say we had nothing to do with any raid, or stealing,' Paul told Higgotty firmly. 'If you want my honest opinion, I think there has been some kind of set-up. But why we have been selected, I can't tell.'

'So why pick on you?' asked Higgotty, puzzlement filling his honest face.

'That's the bit I don't understand,' Paul replied impatiently. 'Doesn't it seem strange or curious that the caller knew so much about us?'

'And where exactly to find us?' Chris added.

'All I know was, I was asked to apprehend you,' replied the policeman. 'I do not question my orders. I merely carry them out.'

'But why was the crowd with you?' persisted Chris.

Higgotty shook his head. 'Beats me. All I know is whoever called the police must have tipped the crowd off as well. How that was done, I can't say. I know my explanation doesn't sound very convincing, but it is the only answer I can think of at this moment.'

'And there were two crowds,' Paul reminded the policeman.

'Yes. PC Biggs is one of my colleagues. Good man— I used to play cricket with him when we were at training college in Hendon. Now, I seem to remember him saying how he had had a tip-off that the suspects were heading off down Back Lane. He was told to block off the one entrance and I was sent to the far end.'

'Didn't you think that strange?' asked Paul.

'Yes, I did. Have you any idea who might have set you up?'

'Zardaka!' Chris said firmly. 'It has to be him. He's the only one with the power round here to do something like that.'

'Zardaka?' The policeman frowned. 'I know that name from somewhere. Never mind! It will all come back to me soon, no doubt.'

'The only problem, as far as I can see, is why Zardaka should want to set up such an elaborate trap to catch us,' Paul objected.

Mr Higgotty consulted his notebook. 'Now then, there are quite a few question I should like to ask you both.'

'Such as?' Paul inquired.

'I have a list of serious allegations. Assault upon a supermarket store detective; attempting to shift your guilt on an innocent member of the public, and then there is a long list of the things you are alleged to have stolen. Do you want me to continue?'

Chris shook his head.

'Perhaps it would help if you were to tell me your story,' suggested the policeman. 'At least that way I get some of these allegations out of the way.'

'Make a statement? That sort of thing?' Chris inquired.

'Yes. That sort of thing.'

Chris and Paul exchanged looks. They both wondered how much of their story the policeman would believe. The more they thought about the events, which had preceded their entry into the garden via the green door, the more improbable everything seemed.

'Well, it was like this...' Chris began.

And as he spoke, the policeman wrote everything down in his rather cramped writing, Paul filling in any missing details, or providing the missing gaps.

Chris had been helping his friend Paul do the shopping for his mother, who was busy with the washing at home. Whilst they were in the supermarket in the centre of town, they had spotted a shabbily dressed man putting groceries into the pockets of his raincoat instead of the wire basket he was carrying. Although both boys felt concerned about the incident, they decided not to do anything. The policeman gave them a rather stern look at this point in the story. Chris and Paul had reached the check-out, just in time to avoid the queue which generally built up there. The young girl at the cash desk looked bored. She inspected the ends of her varnished nails critically and nodded briefly to the boys. Her name was Belinda Frazer. The boys only knew Belinda by sight. She had attended the same school but was much older than them and had left well over a year ago. She nodded to the boys but did not enter into conversation with them. After they had gone through the cash point, Chris half looked back. Belinda was consulting a price list for frozen goods as she attended the next customer. For the first time, he noticed what a good looking girl Belinda was. Her blonde hair was well-groomed and he liked the way she had applied blusher to her cheeks. The store overall didn't do much for her figure, but despite this, she was still attractive girl.

'Hurry up!' Paul snapped. 'Anyone would think you fancied Belinda.'

Chris blushed as he held the door open for his friend.

'Let's get out of here. I hate shopping.'

'Excuse me,' said a harsh voice as they reached the street. Paul paused, supposing that the dark suited stranger wanted to ask him the time, or perhaps the direction of the nearest bus station. He was in for a shock.

'Excuse me, sir,' the man said. 'I think you forgot to pay for some of the items you bought in this store.' The dark suited man grasped him firmly by the elbow.

'What?' gasped Paul staring at the man in astonishment.

'Come on, let's have none of your nonsense!' snapped the man roughly.

'Take your hands off me!' Paul shouted.

'What on earth do you think you're doing?' Chris asked. 'He paid for those goods.'

'I've been watching you both for some time,' the stranger said. He looked around anxiously at the growing crowd, as if not sure which side they were on.

'I'm sure you don't want a scene. Let's go into my office and then we can discuss things properly.'

'But who are you?' Chris demanded. 'And what right have you to question us?'

'Perkins. I'm the store detective. Now, if you'll just step this way.'

His hand was firmly on Paul's elbow.

'But we've paid for everything,' Paul protested. 'You can see my till receipt if you like. Here it is.' He thrust the piece of paper under Perkins' nose. With a sinking heart, Paul realised that he and Chris should have reported the shabbily dressed man as soon as they reached the check-out and not left their worries unattended.

'Oh, we'll check everything if you come with me, sir,' Perkins said sarcastically.

'We know how to deal with your sort.'

'How dare you!' Paul stormed. 'I'm not a thief.'

'Oh, no? Then what are these?' With the finesse of a conjurer performing his latest trick, Perkins pulled out several assorted packets of soup powder from Paul's coat pocket. The boy gasped with surprise.

'Of course,' said the store detective smoothly. 'You are under no obligation to say anything until the police arrive.' He turned and faced Chris. 'I shall have to also ask you to come along as well. I think you both have a great deal of explaining to do.'

When Chris began to protest, but Perkins cut him short. Deftly he flicked open an inside pocket in Chris's coat, whereupon packets of ladies' tights fell out, plus some tubes of toothpaste and sachets of hair shampoo. Chris couldn't quite believe what was happening to him. 'You've got the wrong people! You must believe me!' he managed to croak. He peered through the knot of people, which had gathered around, watching the whole sordid incident. Then he spotted someone familiar.

'That's the man over there! Look!'

Perkins did not look round. He was too experienced to fall for that trick.

'Come along!' he said roughly as he gripped both boys by the arms. 'Let's have no unpleasantness. You are only making things worse for yourselves.'

'But that is the man! He's walking across the street and if we're quick we can catch him.'

'A likely story!' snorted the store detective indignantly. 'You both had better come along with me and

47

help sort this lot out. I'd like to have your names of addresses and then we'll get in touch with the police. You can keep your explanations for them. I've met your sort before. I expect you've both got records as long as my arm.'

Paul felt his face flame with indignation. He exchanged a helpless glance with Chris. They both knew they could never explain the situation properly to Perkins. He just wouldn't listen. Both boys realised that somehow when their attention had been distracted at the check-out, the shabbily dressed man, whoever he was, had planted the packets of soup and ladies' tights on them. That way he could bring suspicion upon the boys without drawing attention to himself.

It was Paul who had signalled what they should do.

'Here! Take your rotten goods!' he said roughly and he thrust the bag of shopping into Perkins arms. 'And here is the other bag!' Chris shouted as he swiped the store detective across the legs with his carrier bag. The dark suited man staggered, losing his grip on Paul's elbow.

'And that's how we came to be in Back Lane, running away from the law,' said Chris.

'Perhaps I should have cautioned you both before you made this statement,' said the policeman. He sighed. 'I'll get it typed up at the station and then you can both sign it.'

'And then?' Chris asked with a worried frown upon his face.

'My superiors will decide whether there will be a court case or not. The supermarket will probably press for one in any case. They like to see people prosecuted, because it deters other would-be-shoplifters from doing the same thing.'

48

'But we aren't shoplifters!' Paul exploded.

'So you keep saying,' said Mr Higgotty indifferently.

'You don't believe us, do you?' said Chris.

'It isn't a case of not believing; It is a case of obeying the law. I do what I am asked to do, not necessarily what I believe in.'

'But surely there are parts of our story which must match up with what you already know,' Paul objected.

'I know that you both hit Perkins, the store detective, with your shopping and that is how he lost his grip on your arm. Your statement matches up with his.'

'But we didn't steal the goods!' Chris exploded. 'They were planted on us by the shabbily dressed man.'

'Perkins makes no mention of this man. He takes the view that you were just trying to divert his attention, so that you could make your escape.'

'I think you are forgetting one important point,' said Paul.

'And what is that?' asked the policeman.

'None of us are going anywhere, unless we can get away from this place.'

'So what do you suggest?'

'That we join forces. At least, until we are out of danger.'

'Meaning, Zardaka?'

'Exactly. We could help each other. If we help you, will you help us?'

'Let me think about that,' mused Mr Higgotty. He consulted his notebook.

'Well now. There might be something in your story about that shabbily dressed man. Maybe I could help you out there, if only you had a witness.'

'But we have a witness!' Paul broke in eagerly.

Chris slapped his head. 'Of course!' he exclaimed. 'Belinda will know if we are telling the truth or not.'

Paul couldn't help sniggering, when he heard the name "Belinda" mentioned.

'That's his fiancée!' he giggled.

Chris glared at his friend angrily.

But Mr Higgotty's face cleared when he realised the significance of this new witness. 'Ah yes! Belinda Frazer, the girl who works on the cash desk in the supermarket.'

'At least you could ask her about us,' said Chris. 'She knows we aren't thieves.'

'All right. I'll check her out,' promised the policeman.

'How on earth do we get out of this garden?' Paul wondered.

Mr Higgotty frowned. 'Funny about that door,' he mused. 'I've been up and down that road a dozen times or more, but I've never seen a door in that wall before. How it has disappeared again, very strange.'

'That's just what we said, before we made our escape through the door,' agreed Chris.

'Most mysterious that,' the policeman mused. 'Do you know, it was also peculiar how strong that door was? It was if it were made from steel, and there were some hefty chaps with me, I can tell you. And as for that wall!' He clicked his tongue disapprovingly. 'Broken glass on top. Don't hold with it myself, a rather cruel practice to my way of thinking'.

The boys nodded in agreement.

'And another funny thing,' the policeman resumed. 'I can't remember anything after climbing on top of that wall. What did happen?'

'You argued with the wizard,' said Paul.

'Ah yes! Circus bloke of some kind. Calls himself Zardaka.'

'You still don't seem to realise that he is a real wizard.'

'So you keep telling me.'

'And he really is dangerous. Don't you remember what he did?'

'Yes. Didn't he do something very odd?'

'Very odd!' Chris agreed. 'He muttered some words'

'And I thought he was swearing. Oh dear! Oh dear!'

'It was some kind of spell. He put a magic spell on you. He turned you into a snake. Can't you remember that?'

Higgotty screwed up his face. 'Come to think of it, I did feel rather strange. Yes! Now it comes back to me! I remember my hands and arms disappearing and then my legs. Next thing I knew, I was sliding down the wall. Funny, but it felt as if I had done that sort of things hundreds of times, natural like, if you know what I mean. Then I must have spent the rest of the time crawling and wriggling around in the undergrowth. Ugh! What a thought! How horrible!' The policeman gave a quick shudder of distaste.

'What happened when the spell wore off? I mean, how did you know you were yourself again?' Paul inquired.

'That is quite odd in its own way,' mused Higgotty. 'You see, I can't remember anything after I slid down the wall, but I do remember the spell wearing off. When that happened I was in the middle of a flower bed. I just sat up suddenly and there I was, me again, I looked a proper sight, I can tell you. Had flowers in my hair and sticking to my

51

uniform. I made a terrible mess of the flowers I'm afraid.' The policeman sighed regretfully.

'Zardaka told us the spell he cast upon you wasn't permanent,' Paul informed him.

'How very nice of him!' said Mr Higgotty sarcastically.

'He would have used a lasting spell on you, if he had had the time,' Chris added.

'That makes it much worse!' said the policeman grimly. 'Assault upon a police officer is a very serious crime, very serious indeed!'

Chris heaved a sigh of exasperation. 'You never learn!'

'What do you mean?' asked Mr Higgotty indignantly.

'Zardaka is using magic to do all these strange things,' Chris explained. 'Magic cannot be fought in any ordinary way. You cannot just go up to Zardaka and arrest him in the same way you would do to any ordinary criminal.'

'So what do I do?'

'You'll have to learn the rules all over again,' said Paul.

'That is, if you want to beat Zardaka at his own game.'

'You cannot expect me to know how to do that,' grumbled PC Higgotty. 'I am here to enforce the law, not to make new laws.'

'It is important to ask ourselves how quickly matters can be put right,' declared Chris.

'That is all very well' began the policeman.

Chris didn't allow him to complete his sentence.

'If we all help each other,' he suggested. 'We might prove more than a match for Zardaka. We are not certain how strong his magic is and that could be one of our greatest problems.'

'We ought to make our escape from the garden our priority,' Paul put in.

'There's my helmet!' shouted the policeman getting to his feet. Sure enough, there was his helmet perched right on top of the wall.

'That is very interesting,' said Chris.

'Interesting, my foot!' growled Mr Higgotty. 'How am I supposed to get it down from there?'

'It marks the spot where the door was!' cried Paul.

'Then we ought to leave it there,' suggested Chris.

'Oh now! I'll never live this down!' groaned the policeman.

'What a disgrace! A police constable without his helmet, stuck in a madman's garden with two very odd people.'

'Well, I like that!' said Paul indignantly. Before he could say anything more, Chris intervened, suddenly realising Mr Higgotty was very upset.

'The constable means no harm, do you?' Chris asked gently.

The policeman shook his head and pulled out his handkerchief.

'Don't upset yourself,' Chris said kindly. Mr Higgotty, strong man though he was, looked as if he was about to cry with mortification at his plight.

'Things might not be as bad as they appear,' suggested Paul.

'The Chief Constable is going to have a great deal to say about this!' sniffed PC Higgotty. 'All those people heard how Zardaka insulted me! They saw him tear up my warrant and all because of you two!'

'Well, I like that!' said Paul for the second time.

'And me, I was only doing my duty,' sniffed poor Higgotty into his spotted handkerchief.

'We'd better leave him on his own for a while,' whispered Chris. 'He'll be all right, but we must give him some time to himself.'

'What exactly is wrong with him?' Paul asked curiously. The policeman's strange behaviour completely mystified him.

'I think it is the effect of the magic wearing off.'

Paul thought about what Chris had said, but as he couldn't think of a better reason for the policeman's odd behaviour, he had to accept it as being the most likely explanation.

'What do you want to do now?' he asked Chris.

'I think we should leave Mr Higgotty here to recover and go back to the house. After all, that is what we originally planned to do.'

Paul looked doubtfully at the policeman.

'Are you afraid of Zardaka?' Chris challenged.

'Not exactly. Only...'

'What?'

'He told us not to wander round his house.'

'But that's exactly what I want to do.'

A Strange Discovery

The house was deserted and everything was unnaturally quiet, except for the occasional tinkle from the mysterious chandeliers. There was no sign of the two shrouded figures who had conducted Chris and Paul to the breakfast table. Paul even tried calling out aloud to them, but there was no reply, only the eerie tinkle of glass against glass, as the chandeliers glittered and sparkled above their heads. Carefully they crept upstairs. They were a little frightened, because they hadn't a clue as to what they were looking for, or what they would find, or even where they should start, but upstairs seemed as good as any other place for making a search. Soon they had reached the long corridor, the one which seemed to stretch for miles. Paul gazed in horror at the task that awaited them. 'Where on earth do we start?' he gasped.

'Here. If that is no good, we think again.'

'But it will take hours!'

'So what?' Chris reasoned. 'We have time on our hands, so let's use it profitably.'

He opened the first door, which was to his right, whilst Paul opened the nearest door to himself, which was the one on the left. Chris's room turned out to be quite ordinary, with a just a view of the garden, the sort of scene one would expect to find. Paul's room, however, turned out to be far more interesting.

'It's a laboratory!' Chris exclaimed excitedly.

'What do you think he uses it for?' asked Paul.

'Workshop. Look at those books and those instruments over there.'

Paul looked around curiously. There certainly was a great deal to see, but he didn't know if any of it would be of use to them in finding a way out of Zardaka's clutches. Test tubes were neatly racked in their hundreds, whilst coloured liquids bubbled and frothed over a mysterious labyrinth of strange flames. Chris suddenly smiled.

'Very pretty, but just a little overdone, don't you think?'

'How do you mean?' asked Paul.

'This stuff is only here to impress the likes of you and me. It really doesn't mean very much. Look at this book for example. What do you think of it?'

Paul took the book. The dusty pages were beginning to crack and flake with age. The faded writing was difficult to make out, but Paul fancied he could make out one of two of the spells there.

'What do you think?'

'What do I think?' Paul echoed. 'You seem to be the expert in these matters. What do you think?'

'Mumbo-jumbo. That's all it is. Mumbo-jumbo! Pure rubbish, put here for our benefit. All this,' said Chris, with a sweep of his hand. 'Was put here to show the unwary how wonderful and powerful Zardaka is. It doesn't seem to make sense, and it won't take me in one little bit.'

As they closed the door behind them, two green eyes followed them. Patch, the wizard's servant cat, had been left to keep an eye on things whilst Zardaka was out on business. 'How very interesting!' Patch murmured to himself. 'I didn't realise the human child possessed such intellect. Zardaka will be most interested when he hears this.'

Unaware that they had been observed by Patch, Chris and Paul continued their search. Most of the rooms were very ordinary and not of great interest. Sometimes, a room would be bare, or it would be filled with furniture. Other rooms might contain just a table, or maybe a couple of stools, or the odd chair. It was most disappointing, because the view from the window was the same stretch of garden. It was as if Zardaka wanted them to start believing that they were opening the same door, time after time. When they looked back, they could see the distance they had travelled. After much hard searching, they came to room which was completely different from the others they had visited.

'At last!' moaned Paul. 'This must be the hundredth door we've looked through today!'

The room was well furnished and much larger than any of the other rooms. Books lined the whole of one side of the room. Chris took down a book, intending to search through it, but Paul called urgently to him. 'I say! Come and look at this!'

With a sigh Chris carefully replaced the book back in its right place and made his way over to where Paul was standing quivering with excitement.

'Well, what is it?'

'A door! Almost hidden by this curtain.'

'How extraordinary!' exclaimed Chris.

'I was looking at these paintings on the wall,' Paul explained, 'where I suddenly noticed this recess. When I lifted the curtain, I found this door. Is it locked?'

'There is only one way to find out the answer to that,' said Chris. He turned the cut glass door knob slowly, and the door opened smoothly and silently to his touch.

Cautiously they entered the adjoining room. Chris paused for a moment to listen, but nothing stirred, only a clock on the wall partially disturbed the silence with its ponderous tick. A rich carpet enveloped their feet, and a heavy cloying scent filled the air, much to Paul's disgust. Expensive furniture was arranged carefully around the room. Exquisite taste had been exercised in choosing the priceless painting which hung from the walls. Chris peeped furtively behind one of the heavy velvet curtains, which almost obscured the tall windows, but there was nothing lurking there to disturb the calm. There was one odd feature about the room, however. Strange Eastern ornaments lay everywhere. They littered the room, like the playthings discarded by some pampered child. Paul spent some time staring at the ornaments, whilst Chris wandered off on his own. As Chris moved across the room a fly buzzed suddenly and angrily against a window pane, frantically trying to escape the lush surroundings, its shrill throbbing contrasted sharply with the sombre ticking of the clock. Chris moved closer, intent on opening the window, so that the fly could escape. To his surprise the room overlooked the same pine forest he had seen that morning from his own window. He knew there was something odd about this, because the room was on the wrong side of the house and, in normal circumstances, could not overlook the forest. Paul wandered over to the marble mantelpiece.

He gazed at the gold candlesticks. The stems were curiously fashioned, so they resembled the trunks of oak trees, with ivy tendrils clinging to the rough bark. He turned with a sigh and made his way over to a table by the window. Purple petals lay across the dark varnish. They had fallen from the dead flowers which stood stiff and brittle in the cut glass vase. But he received a terrible shock, as he turned away from looking at the decayed flowers. Two yellow eyes suddenly bored into his. Paul almost screamed with terror, but just managed to stop himself in time. He felt his heart bang painfully against his ribs. A white owl stood on a small stand near to the table. It looked alive, but Chris informed Paul that it was more likely to have been stuffed, or preserved in some way. Meanwhile, Chris had spotted something of equal interest. He had come across a model of a Chinese junk, with fierce, rather cruel looking sailors, or maybe they were pirates? Anyway, Chris would not have fancied his chances if he had happened to meet them. He turned away. More wooden figures stood on the far side of the room. They looked like soldiers, but they were unlike any soldiers Chris had ever seen before. They stood before him in warlike poses, gripping their weapons eagerly, glazing unblinkingly with their cold sapphire eyes., Chris couldn't help shivering. There was something cruel and unpleasant about the whole room. It was as if something terrible could happen at any time.

'Let's go,' he said abruptly to Paul.

'Wait a bit. I haven't seen everything,' objected Paul.

'We are wasting time here.'

'You really are a spoil sport! This is the first good room we have seen, and you want to leave already.'

'Perhaps. All I know is that I can smell danger.'

'You must have a remarkably good nose. All I can smell is that awful perfume.'

'Yes. I've been wondering about that perfume. It could be the only clue in the room. The other things could have been left here on purpose, but the perfume could have been an accident.'

'What is it?' Chris asked.

'There is someone in the room with us. I can hear something.'

Patch, who had hidden himself behind some rich furnishings, got ready to spring, should either of the two boys move in his direction, but his nerves suddenly relaxed as he saw Paul lead Chris to the other side of the room, where a velvet curtain hid yet another room.

'Aaaah!' Patch breathed. His work completed, he crept away to report his findings to Zardaka.

'How very strange!' exclaimed Chris, as he and Paul made their way into the third room.

'Hush!' I think she is sleeping.'

'Who?'

'Why, that girl over there.'

The girl's long golden hair would not have disgraced one of the old legendary German princesses. If she had been standing upright, instead of lying down, her hair would have reached her waist. As it was, the exotic tresses fell about her face in a shimmering mass, spilling over on to the pillow on which she rested her head.

'Who is she?' Chris wanted to know.

'How on earth should I know?' Paul replied indignantly.

'I've never seen her before; perhaps she is some princess the wizard has stolen from some far-off kingdom. After all, that's what used to happen in the olden days, you know. Why don't you ask her who she is, when she wakes up?'

'She is very beautiful,' Chris said wistfully.

The girl gave a long sigh, almost as if she was about to wake, but only her eyelashes fluttered momentarily, and then her deep regular breathing continued.

'There! You almost woke her,' Paul said crossly.

'I like that! You've been making enough noise yourself, you know.'

'Huh!' Paul exclaimed in deep disgust.

Chris ignored Paul and went nearer the girl. She wore a plain black gown of velvet, with white lace at the sleeves and throat. A gold medallion hung from a chain about her neck. On the third finger of her left hand was a ring, with a design which matched that of the medallion. Her feet revealed stockings of the finest silk, and a pair of discarded silver slippers lay at the foot of the couch.

'She should be able to help us,' Chris said decisively.

'How do you know? Have you asked her? If she could help us, she would have helped herself a long time ago,' Paul said a trifle tartly. He added spitefully: 'Perhaps she isn't a prisoner at all.'

Chris paused in his examination of the girl's face.

'I hadn't thought of that,' he admitted.

At that moment the girl woke up She opened her mouth as if she was about to scream, but the kindly smiles of the two boys seemed to reassure her that she was in no danger. She sat up on the couch, smoothed down her dress and hair, before pushing her feet back into her slippers.

Chris, who was completely captivated by the girl, told their story, occasionally interrupted by Paul, who kept putting in the little bits which Chris left out. The girl listened with great interest.

'Now it is your turn,' said Chris when he had finished.

'My name is Stella Holmes,' the girl began. 'I am not a princess, or anyone very special. I am a prisoner of the wizard, Zardaka. At school I never believed in such things as wizards, but now I know differently. One should never laugh at the improbable, or impossible.'

'So, what happened to you?' Chris asked. 'How did Zardaka catch you?'

'Well,' Stella explained. 'One day I was playing with my friends in a field, not far from home, when a lovely black kitten came gambolling across the grass to where we were playing. My friends and I ran after the kitten, but it was too fast for us. It led us away from the field to a small wood, and there my friends were separated from me. I now know it was a very foolish thing to do. You see, I continued to search for the kitten on my own, instead of going back to the meadow.'

'And so you went deeper into the wood?' Paul inquired.

'Yes. And each time I thought I would catch the kitten, it moved just a little further out of reach.'

Stella paused, as if she were afraid to continue.

'And then what happened?' Chris prompted.

She took a deep breath, as if anxious to get rid of the next part of her story in one go.

'And then this perfectly innocent kitten suddenly changed into this terribly tall man with a long white beard and a pointed hat upon his head. Ridiculous! I could hardly believe it. Before I could say a word, or shout, he seized me by the arm and here I have been ever since, only seeing him and his servant, Patch.'

'Patch?' chorused the boys in amazement. 'Who's he?'

'Don't say you haven't met Patch?' asked Stella in astonishment. They shook their heads. 'Patch is Zardaka's servant, a black cat, very sly, very evil, always telling tales out of spite to get me into trouble, regardless of whether I have done anything or not. If trying to escape is wrong, tell me what else a prisoner is supposed to do? Then there are those two shrouded servants, the ones without faces, who clean the place up from time to time.'

'We've seen them,' Chris interrupted. 'They are positively creepy.'

'They are harmless,' the girl said. 'You needn't worry.'

'But why does the wizard want you?' asked Paul.

Stella shrugged. 'Zardaka is always telling me to look my very best. He supplies me with all sorts of pretty clothes and tells me it is all for his Grand Plan.'

'And what is this Grand Plan?' Chris inquired.

'He intends to take over our world and make slaves of the people.'

'Are you going to help him to do this?' Chris asked aghast.

Stella gave him a pitying sort of look.

'You mean, do I want to help him? The answer to that question is a very definite "no". But in real terms I have no choice, I have to help him, otherwise I have no other means of escaping this house and garden.'

'Does Zardaka really need your help?' Chris asked.

63

Stella looked puzzled.

'With all his powers, surely he doesn't really need you,' Paul explained.

'I'm not sure about that. All I know is that I have to operate some machine. It looks a bit like a computer, but not the sort of computer we have at school, if you understand what I mean. It is a great big complex machine, with loads of terminals and mysterious gadgets, which I don't pretend to understand. Zardaka says he needs me, because it is impossible for him to be everywhere on the day he takes over the world.'

'That's a relief,' muttered Paul.

'What else did you expect?' Stella asked wearily. 'He says he will make me Queen of Europe, as a reward for helping him.'

'What do you suppose he expect to accomplish with this mad plan?' Chris asked.

'Domination of the entire universe, that is his ultimate plan.'

Chris and Paul exchanged glances.

'Look, I know it sounds ridiculous, but Zardaka is deadly serious.'

'Sorry, but I can't take any of this seriously,' said Chris.

Stella frowned deeply. 'You really have to believe in what Zardaka says, otherwise you will be in deep danger. Zardaka can do exactly as he pleases. I don't think there is one person on earth who could stop him.'

'What if you refuse to co-operate?' Paul wanted to know.

Stella shook her head doubtfully.

'I think Zardaka would just find someone else. You see, he is jealous of the power of the Grand Oval. Oh, I can see you've heard of the Grand Oval.'

'Yes, I seem to remember the Grand Oval being mentioned, just before Zardaka put a spell on Higgotty the policeman,' Chris agreed.

'But what is this Grand Oval?' asked Paul.

'The Grand Oval is a group of magicians who keep the balance of power between them. In short, they are the ones who control the universe. Zardaka is determined to show them just who is the master magician.'

'Have you ever tried to escape?' Chris asked.

Stella laughed. 'Yes. I've tried to escape. Many times. Each time I've been hunted down and brought back.'

'How did you escape?'

'Once I tried to get through the pine forest, but Zardaka was too quick for me.'

Paul and Chris exchanged dubious glances.

Stella intercepted the look.

'If you don't believe me, have you tried looking through any of the other windows?'

'Yes and they seem to be worse than the pine forest,' Paul admitted. 'You won't believe what I saw from my window. It must have been some sort of joke.'

'What was outside your window?' asked Stella.

'A steep cliff with a raging sea at the bottom.'

'But it didn't stop me.'

Chris and Paul stared at Stella in disbelief.

'How do you mean?' asked Chris.

'You don't know the half of it,' Stella said calmly, not at all put out by their disbelieving looks. 'I even tried to get through the jungle once and was nearly eaten by the crocodiles there'

'Ugh!' shuddered Paul, who hated reptiles.

'You see,' Stella explained. 'Each window overlooks something different!'

'But we know that!' Chris exclaimed impatiently. 'Just exactly what are you trying to tell us?'

'My! You really are dense!' Stella said sharply. 'Don't you see? Zardaka wants to take over the world, so what does he do? He builds a house which overlooks every part of the world.'

'That's it!' shouted Paul. 'Some windows overlook deserts, other jungles.'

'Or snowy tundra regions' Chris added.

'Mountains, valleys, Norwegian forests,' continued Paul.

'Volcanoes,' Stella finished for both.

'Yes. We saw that. Nearly got caught by the lava,' Chris said grimly.

'So you see,' Stella said. 'Everything is real. A window for each part of the world, and no possible escape for us in sight.'

'How did Zardaka bring you back?' Paul asked.

'He simply used his powers and came after me,' Stella explained. 'It was awful! The crocodiles had me cornered. I didn't know a jungle could be so frightful.'

'It must have been a terrifying experience for you,' Chris said sympathetically.

'The snakes were the worst. There were some great big ones, as thick as your arm.'

'Don't groaned Paul growing pale. 'I don't want to hear anymore!'

'What's wrong with him?' Stella asked Chris.

'Paul hates reptiles of any kind,' Chris explained.

'Sorry, Paul,' Stella apologised.

'So what did Zardaka say to you, after you tried to escape?' Chris inquired.

'He said that I deserved to be left to my fate and the next time I tried to escape he would let me die.'

'Surely you didn't try to escape after that?' Paul asked.

'Oh yes I did! Many times. I tried the desert. It was so hot. I turned back. Luckily, Zardaka never found out about that.'

'Was it really that bad?' Paul asked. 'I mean, despite the heat, couldn't you have escaped?'

Stella shook her head.

'You can't imagine what it was like. For a start there were all these flies. Secondly, I only had a silly ornamental bottle in which to carry water. I would have died if I hadn't turned back.'

'What did you do next?'

'I tried the snowy plain, do you know the one? I nearly froze to death that time, because I only had my summer clothes. Zardaka saved me again. He said that I ought to be grateful and that perhaps I would learn to be obedient.'

'And were you obedient?'

'Certainly not! I tried the sea scene next. It was calm, and I think Zardaka left a boat there on purpose, just to teach me a lesson. A terrible storm blew up and I thought I was going to drown. As it was, I was terribly seasick. As I said, I think Zardaka caused the storm, just to show who was boss.'

'How did you get back?'

'Zardaka must have relented. He sent Mista the Owl, another of his servants, to bring me back. I was ill for a week after that, but Zardaka didn't care. He said it served me right and when would I learn that it was useless to try escaping.'

'You must have some value to him, or he wouldn't bother to bring you back each time,' Chris said.

'Perhaps. I think he wants me to respect him for rescuing me, but he is wrong. He forgets that he brought me here, against my will. In every attempted escape I have made, he has been morally responsible for my near death.'

'Are you still trying to escape?' Chris wanted to know.

Stella sighed. 'No. I have given up trying to escape. It all seems so pointless. I rarely walk in the garden now.' She sounded so doleful, the boys felt uncomfortable. To make things worse, Stella looked as if she were about to burst into tears. Then she pulled herself together with an effort.

'You must be hungry,' she said. 'I was forgetting that I am your host.' Rising to her feet, Stella clapped her hands. Within a few minutes the shrouded figures had laid out a wonderful meal.

For a long time no one felt very much like speaking, mouths and hands being industriously employed. Stella, eventually, broke the silence by saying: 'By the way. Where is that policeman friend of yours?'

'I was forgetting about him. How about you Chris?' said Paul.

'Higgotty will be all right, providing he stays out of sight,' said Chris.

'Zardaka often forgets about people, once he has put a spell on them,' Stella told them. 'Perhaps he has forgotten your Mr Higgotty.'

'How very convenient of Zardaka to forget about people, once he has cast a spell on them,' said Paul sarcastically.

'You know, if your Mr Higgotty did remain out of sight, he could be a great help to us,' Stella told the boys. 'We need to find him and bring him here.'

'What about the other members of the Grand Oval, would they be able to help us?' Paul asked.

'Yes, that would be all right, if only we could contact them,' said Stella.

'How does Zardaka feel towards them?' Paul wanted to know.

'How do you mean?'

'I mean, would they help us against another member of the Oval?'

Stella thought for a moment. 'Zardaka's not exactly frightened of them, if that is what you mean. But he is, shall we say, wary of upsetting them directly.'

It was at that moment the curtain covering the entrance to the room was torn aside, and there, to everyone's horror, stood Zardaka!

'Ha!' he purred, rubbing his long bony fingers together.

'The strangers meet! How very convenient!'

'And what exactly do you mean by that?' Stella demanded. She was very pale and had risen to her feet.

'Silence!' hissed the wizard. 'You forget yourself. I will ask the questions. Now! What have you all been up to?'

'I won't be quiet!' Stella declared. 'You have kept me prisoner long enough.'

'You will be silent!' the wizard thundered. 'Patch! Come here at once!'

'So! You have set Patch to spy upon us during the time you were away, have you?' cried Stella angrily.

'Your friends, it seems, have abused the rules of hospitality!' snarled Zardaka. 'Patch! Patch! You rascal! Come here at once!'

'Coming, Master!' said a faint voice in the distance.

'But what have we done to offend you?' Chris asked in an innocent voice.

'You have found out too much for your own good. You have disobeyed my specific instructions and wishes by wandering around the house, peeking and prying into places where you had no right to go.'

'Come off it, Zardaka!' Chris said angrily. 'You are holding this girl, Stella, prisoner against her wishes.'

'What do you know of her wishes?' asked the wizard contemptuously.

'Surely Stella has the right to leave, if she wants to?' Paul said reasonably.

'That is not for you, or the girl, to decide. I have a specific reason for everything I do,' said the wizard loftily.

'What about those who are unable to leave?' Paul objected.

'Surely they have the right to escape?'

'No one escapes me,' said Zardaka with a frown.

'Here I am, Master,' said Patch coming into the room. Patch was a large black cat with cruel, crafty, green eyes, which stared at everyone without blinking.

'Tell me what you know, Patch—every word—I want these people to hear.'

'I will, Master. Everything I know.'

'Traitor!' hissed Stella between her clenched teeth. She had gone very pale and gave the cat a withering look of contempt.

'Silence!' commanded the wizard. 'My servants are loyal to me, and answerable only to myself. They are not traitors. But if they become untrue…' Zardaka let his last sentence fade into significant silence. Everyone gave a shudder of horror. They all knew very well what the wizard would do to those who served him badly, or betrayed his trust. Zardaka never needed to make any pronouncement explicit, he relied on implication alone.

'Speak on, Patch!' ordered Zardaka.

'Very well, Master. The boys, Paul and Christopher, came into the house from the garden.'

'Had they breakfasted first?'

'Yes, Master.'

'Interesting!'

Then they came back into the house, after walking in the garden.'

'Had they spoken to anyone in the garden?'

Both Chris and Paul felt their hearts sink into their boots when Zardaka rapped out this question. The wizard's snake-like eyes held Patch's frightened look in a hypnotic gaze, as if intent on sucking out the truth from the depths of the wretched cat's soul.'

'No one, Master, they couldn't have, there was no one in the garden at the time.'

71

'You are sure of this?'

Patch nodded.

Chris felt himself breathe more easily. A flush of colour came back into Stella's waxy cheeks, and Paul looked a trifle less shaky.

'Good!' said the wizard.

So, thought Chris, the all-powerful Zardaka does not know everything. The cat had not been aware of the policeman's presence in the garden. So long as PC Higgotty did not try to regain his helmet, or do something equally silly, he would remain undetected. This could be useful to all of them.

'And what happened next, Patch?'

'They made their way upstairs.'

'And what was their object in doing that?'

'They were trying to find out the secrets of the house.'

'Ah!'

'When they arrived upstairs, I was hiding in the laboratory.'

Chris and Paul exchanged a quick glance.

'At first they were busy looking in the other rooms.'

'And what did they find?'

'There is nothing to find there, Master. You said yourself…'

'Yes! Yes! I know what I said! Go on!' snapped Zardaka. Patch flinched at the sound of the wizard's angry voice.

'At first,' he continued hurriedly. 'They appeared to be impressed by the things we have in the laboratory, all those books, the test tubes, phials, glasses.'

'I know, I know!' thundered the wizard. 'There is no need to give me a complete inventory. I know exactly what the room contains.'

He turned and faced Chris.

'So, what did you find in the book?' he snapped.

'Old spells, old rhymes and old potions, Zardaka. Cures for warts, digging for gold under blue moons, to say nothing of rainbows and dancing in fairy rings. All that rot! A bit out-of-date, if you ask me.'

'Was that the book?' Zardaka demanded of Patch.

'Yes, Master. That was the one.'

'I see,' said the wizard slowly. 'And you looked in no other book?'

'What books?' Chris asked scornfully. 'I am not interested in crocks of gold at the end of rainbows, are you?'

'I most certainly am not,' said the wizard coldly. 'You are sure you looked in no other book?'

Chris shook his head.

'Then I must congratulate you on your superior knowledge in those areas to which we wizards are so ignorant. And yet,' Zardaka continued, in his smooth silky voice, 'you both told me that you were not connected with magic when you entered the garden. Do you now inform me that you were both lying?'

'We are not connected with magic,' Chris said firmly.

'That is a truthful answer,' Zardaka agreed.

'Then answer a question of mine,' challenged Chris boldly.

'Very well then,' said the wizard. 'Ask your question.'

'How long do you intend to keep us prisoner here?' Chris inquired.

73

'I cannot prevent anyone from entering my garden, as you and your friend did. Nor can I prevent people, like Stella, chasing after kittens.'

'But that doesn't alter the fact that you took me away from my friends and family against my will!' protested Stella.

'And yet,' shot back the wizard. 'I do not stop you leaving.'

'But you do! Every time I try to escape, you bring me back.'

'And you try my patience by your continual scheming and plotting. So, for the time being, we shall leave things as they are. This will give you all time to think things over. Do not think you can leave without my permission. Escape is impossible. I shall return later to inform you of my plans, and what I shall expect you all to do for me. Patch will convey my orders to you. It would be as well if you tried to obey them.' With a sweep of his cloak, Zardaka and Patch left the room.

'Hmn! An interesting cat,' said Paul.

Stella shuddered. 'I think he's perfectly horrible! And I've seen far more of him than you have.'

'How much do you think Patch heard?' Paul asked.

'Not much, but enough,' Chris replied.

'That's Patch all over,' said the girl. 'Always spying and listening and carrying tales back to his Master.'

'The first thing we are going to do is take a little walk. By that, I mean Paul and myself.'

'Not in the wood,' Stella objected. 'You'll never get through it. I've tried.'

'I'm not so sure about that. If we do things my way, I think we might succeed. You must remember, Zardaka thinks it is impossible to escape from his house.'

'He's right,' Stella murmured.

'All right! So we keep him thinking that way.'

'Do you have a plan, or are you just guessing?' asked Paul.

'I'm not really sure. We need to look around and try and find a way out of this mess. We know now that it is not just a question of escaping, but also we have a duty in stopping Zardaka from taking over the world.'

'How about your policeman friend, Mr Higgotty?' Stella asked.

'Ah! This is where you come in,' Chris told her. 'I want you to contact him. Higgotty could be our ace card, especially as Zardaka doesn't know about him.'

Chris turned to Stella. 'Keep the window open for our return.'

'You will be careful, won't you?' pleaded Stella. 'Promise me you'll do nothing reckless.'

'Of course we won't,' Chris reassured her. 'Keep a look out for Higgotty.'

Stella came forward and kissed both Chris and Paul on the cheek, much to their embarrassment.

'Don't worry about me; I'm going to look for Mr Higgotty.'

Into the Forest

Chris asked Paul to help him with the window. For a few anxious moment they struggled to get the window open wide enough to allow Chris to make his way through. 'Come on!' he ordered, once he was standing safely on the narrow ledge, which ran underneath the window. 'See the bush down there?'

'What about it?'

'Use it to cushion your fall. I'll jump first, and then you.'

Despite his doubts, Paul closed his eyes and did as he was told. Chris dragged him to his feet and rather roughly began to propel him towards the distant forest.

'We've no time to admire the scenery,' Chris told him.

Together, they lurched across the tussock meadow, which stretched from the wizard's house to the dark fastness of the forest. Once they had reached the edge of the forest, they pushed their way deep into the undergrowth, panting and gasping for breath, fighting the branches and wet leaves which slapped against their faces. Several times Paul tried to stop for a rest, but Chris grabbed him firmly by the arm and dragged him even further into the undergrowth.

'Keep going!' he hissed through clenched teeth. 'This is no place to stop.'

At last they reached a spot where the trees completely blocked out the sunlight. It was very dark and very quiet, with only the sound of an occasional insect to disturb the peace. An aromatic scent from the evergreen trees cast its heavy perfume all around them. Paul sank gratefully on to a convenient bed of pine needles.

'We can't stay here long,' Chris warned.

'Just a little rest,' Paul pleaded.

By late afternoon they were deep into the forest. The boys travelled more slowly now. Occasional shafts of sunlight pierced the dark mass of trees, reminding them of that other world which existed outside this harsh green world. The silence was broken from time to time by the drip-drip sound of water falling through pine needles. But even this reassuring sound could not completely dispel the slightly eerie feeling of being constantly watched. Paul didn't like that creepy sensation one little bit; he jumped at every sudden sound, such as the crackle of a twig or branch. In the end Chris lost patience with him and told him to be quiet, or he would leave him to find his own way through the forest. Paul gazed into the gloom of the forest, and promised to be brave, adding that his nerves couldn't stand much more. Gradually, they both became quite used to the forest and for a considerable time walked in silence, each wrapped in his own private thoughts. It was the sound of a bird singing that broke their solitude. They stopped to listen. The bird trilled again, cutting through the silence with a series of silvery notes that glistened like the bright afternoon sunlight, which occasionally forced its way between the close growing trees. The bird began to hop from branch to branch, its song bubbling in its throat, sounding just as if it were addressing them, as it made its

77

way from twig to twig, performing a curious frantic dance. 'Is that bird trying to tell us something?' asked Paul.

The bird called out impatiently and danced up and down.

'I think we are supposed to follow,' said Chris.

'It could be a trap,' Paul suggested.

Chris shrugged. 'That's a chance we'll have to take.'

They began to follow the bird as it hopped and fluttered ahead of them. From time to time, the bird would break into a short song. The rich sobbing notes sounded rather like rain breaking gently against a window pane. Unfortunately, the boys had no time to listen, because they had to walk quickly to keep up with the bird. Once or twice they almost lost sight of the bird. The first time this happened, Paul thought they had been tricked, but the bird called out impatiently, as if ordering them to hurry up.

The bird was blue, no bigger than a robin, with bright black eyes, a yellow beak and matching feet and legs. It seemed to be in a great hurry and gave nervous glances to the right and left from time to time, as if it expected danger to arrive at any moment.

'I only hope we can find our own way back,' Paul panted, and then he tripped for what seemed like the hundredth time, as he redoubled his efforts to keep up with both Chris and the bird. At last they came to a steep bank and their journey became slightly easier, because the trees tended to be more spaced out. Even so, their breath came in great whistling gasps, and it took all their efforts to keep up with the bird. Just when they thought they could climb no further without a rest, they reached a rocky ledge. Chris wiped the sweat from his face with a rather grimy handkerchief.

'Can't see much here,' he said.

'The bird!' Paul gasped. 'Why! It's flown away!'

'Well! Of all the mean tricks!' Chris exploded. 'What are we supposed to do now?'

'Go home, if we can find the way,' Paul mumbled gloomily. They both looked half-heartedly at the rocky cliff which faced them, thinking about the dirty trick which the bird had played upon them.

'Blowed if I know what we are supposed to be looking for,' said Paul.

'Hang on!' cried Chris. 'There's a blue feather lying here. Could it be a clue? Here! What is this?' He pulled aside a curtain of greenery from the slab of rock facing them.

'A cave!' breathed Paul in amazement. 'So this is what the bird wanted us to find.'

'Then we had better explore,' reasoned Chris. 'And we ought to be quick about it. Judging by the rate that bird disappeared, it makes me think that there must be some kind of danger about this place.'

'I agree,' Paul said.

They ducked their heads under the curtain of greenery and entered the cave.

'Now what?' Paul wondered.

'Straight on,' said Chris.

It was cold inside the cave. There was something horrible about the wet slimy darkness, compared with the bright sunshine outside. Chris and Paul felt as if something, or someone had suddenly wrapped cold clay around them. They kept close to one another, each frightened that the other would suddenly disappear, leaving the other to fend against the hidden dangers alone.

It was quiet at first, but somewhere in the distance they heard water dripping into what sounded like a deep well. 'A bit cold, isn't it?' Paul shivered.

'Better watch your step,' Chris advised. 'Whatever it is that water is falling into, I don't like the sound of it. Sounds pretty deep to me.'

Nevertheless, they began to inch their way forwards through the ever-increasing darkness in the direction of the dripping water. Eventually, they came across a long passage, possibly formed by an underground stream several centuries before. The air was decidedly damper than it had been previously and the floor and walls of the passage were cold and slippery to the touch.

'I don't like it,' said Paul. 'Let's go back.'

'Just a little bit further,' Chris urged. His voice sounded hollow in the tunnel. 'We ought to find out what is at the end of this passage.'

The path began to slope downwards. At first it was a gentle descent and then by degrees it grew steeper and steeper. They rounded another corner and the sound of dripping water became louder. The air felt icy and the two friends began to shiver so much that their teeth sounded like knives and forks being rattled together. The water laden air began to seep into their clothes, and the darkness loaned its own suggestion of foreboding. it was as if they were being slowly drawn into some evil well or whirlpool, which would eventually suck them down forever. There, in the bowels of the earth, they would perish in the coldness of the horrible blackness.

'Ugh!'

'What is wrong?' Chris asked in terror.

'My feet—they are covered in water!'

'What! Oh goodness! So are mine!'

'Let's pack it in, before we are both drowned.'

'Hold on!' called Chris. 'I think there is something on this ledge beside me which might help us.'

His fingers scrabbled for a few moments against the ledge his hands had found in the darkness.

'Ah! A stub of a candle, I think. Strange. I wonder who left this here?'

'Never mind that! Light the wretched thing!' Paul demanded. 'I'm not very much interested in who left the candle stub there. I'm more interested in finding out where we are.'

'All right! All right!'

Chris felt in his pocket and to his delight found the box of matches he had purchased during their visit to the supermarket. Then, much to Paul's relief, a match flared and Chris had successfully lighted the stub. The light it gave was feeble, but it was enough for their needs. The cave, or cavern, as it turned out to be, was quite low where they were standing, but later it widened out and stretched away into the blackness. Instead of a floor surface, the ground on which they were standing had given way to a great black lake, with hundreds of stalactites hanging from the ceiling of the cavern. Water dripped from their tips into the cold dark water.

'Limestone!' Chris exclaimed in amazement.

'What?'

'Don't you remember? We were told about caves like this in geography. This hill must be made from limestone, how otherwise would this cavern have been formed? These stalactites must be hundreds of years old, if not thousands, or maybe millions. Look over there. Every so many years a stalactite will join with a stalagmite to create a perfect pillar. Do you see that great big one over there?'

'Yes. It is like being in a church.'

'You're right! Look how these pillars stretch themselves upwards into the darkness.'

'I wish we could have just a little more light, then I could see how it joins with the roof.'

The boys stood gazing in wonder at the incredible underworld they had stumbled upon. The ghostly yellow light from the candle was reflected by the black waters and the limestone shapes stood out in sharp relief, like the teeth of some ferocious monster waiting to devour the world. But this monster made no sound and so presented no immediate danger. Beneath their feet the gloomy water gurgled ceaselessly, almost touching their toes, whilst the damp air ran its clammy fingers through their hair, touching their lips with its soggy embrace. Away in the distance a feeble light appeared, not much stronger than the light from their candle-flame. The pin-prick of light twinkled, then disappeared, before flickering back to life again. Chris gazed in surprise, then rubbed his eyes in disbelief.

'It looks like some kind of boat,' he said,' he said. 'What do you suppose it could be?'

'I hope it isn't Zardaka up to one of his tricks,' said Chris with a frown.

They stepped further from the water's edge, so that it no longer lapped against their feet. The candle stub was burning more feebly now. The distant light continued to approach them. As it drew nearer, Paul could see that Chris had been right; it was a boat of some sort, with a bright lantern at the prow. The lantern threw shivering reflections across the surface of the lake. Suddenly a fish leapt and shot like a silver flame back into the water. Paul gave a gulp of fright. The waves turned luminous, almost as if a million glow-worms had invaded them. Paul peered more closely at the water and saw that fishes caused the light; their tails appeared to made from strands of sunlight. The lantern bobbed invitingly as the boat continued to move across the lake towards them. It weaved slowly, but expertly between the great pillars of limestone, carefully avoid the limestone teeth, which threatened to tear the bottom out of the vessel.

'There's no one on board!' cried Chris in amazement.

'Then how did the boat find its way here without hitting the rocks?'

'Beats me. Ouch!' he suddenly exclaimed.

'What's wrong?' Paul asked with alarm.

'This candle stub is melting fast and burning my fingers. I'm going to have to put it down somewhere. Gosh! What a mess!' Chris managed to put the spluttering candle carefully on a convenient ledge, so that he could lick his burnt fingers.

'That decides it!' Paul said in a decided sort of voice.

'We'll have to go on now. Besides, we have no light so we have no choice. We'll just have to get in that boat, and let it take it where it wants to.'

'Good!' Chris looked relieved. 'I couldn't face going back through that cave. Far too creepy.'

The mysterious boat drew nearer. It was much larger than it had appeared from a distance. It was a bit like a rowing boat, only wider and somewhat longer, with padded seats and a canopy of some rich material to protect its passengers. There were some green cushions to recline upon, but no oars, or any way of steering the boat. Nor was there any name painted on the side of the craft, only a simple design picked out in gold, rather like the one engraved upon Stella's medallion. The vessel stopped beside them, bobbing quietly on the water. It was just as if the boat expected them to board. Gingerly the boys stepped board. The boat began to rock wildly.

'Hello!' exclaimed Chris, scrambling to his feet in alarm.

'We seem to be off. This boat didn't waste much time, did it?'

'I wonder what will happen to us now?' Paul asked gloomily.

'I wouldn't worry about that until we reach our destination,' Chris replied. 'Just look at the speed we are going!'

The blackness stretched out on either side of them. There wasn't much they could really look at, except the odd stalactite or stalagmite, but that was about it. After a while, the journey became very boring, especially after the hectic adventures, they had so recently sampled. Chris curled himself upon on one of the cushions at the stern of the boat, and lulled by the motion of the water was soon fast asleep. Paul, despite his initial caution, could feel his eyelids drooping with fatigue.

Dawn came slowly, with the pink waves extended their trembling exploring blades of light into the blackness. Like searching fingers they relentlessly began to comb the gloom, lightening the waves here and there, so they resembled bright cellophane. Chris and Paul looked anxiously at each other, faces shiny with the bright reflections of the water. The bright colours appeared to be an awful warning of the dangers which were about to come. A light breeze began to stir the waves and the boat began to rock. The motion was pleasant enough to begin with, but within minutes of the first gentle rocking movement, the vessel began to jump about with ever increasing violence. It was a bit like riding an unruly horse, except that a rider does have some control over a horse; Chris and Paul had no control over their boat, because they had no oars, or any method of steering. In any case, what good would oars have been to two people who could not sail, or even row a boat?

'I feel sick!' groaned Paul holding his stomach.

'So do I, but there is nothing we can do about it.'

The storm broke with full force. It was so fierce that Paul soon forgot about feeling sick. Thunder and lightning ripped the sky, sending a shrieking wind about their heads. The protective canopy was torn away. They saw it winging its way across the sky, like some awful black crow. With nothing to shield them from the elements, the cold rain flew into their faces, half-blinding them, whilst water began to spill over the sides of the little craft, saturating them. Paul somehow found a wooden bowl, which they used between them to get the worst of the storm-water out of the boat, otherwise they might have sunk.

Just when it seemed they would be unable to stop the little boat from foundering, the storm started to show some signs of dying away. It had lasted the best part of an hour. Chris rubbed his eyes in disbelief. For the first time they could see exactly where they were since boarding the vessel.

'I don't believe it!' he exclaimed. 'We're out of that cave, on the open sea somewhere.'

The sun came out and quickly dried their clothes.

'Thank goodness for the sun!' exclaimed Paul. 'Now, if only there was something to eat, I would be completely happy.'

'You and your talk about food!' said Chris a trifle scornfully.

'Aren't you hungry?'

'I'd rather have something to drink.'

'Let's have a good look round the boat then.'

Despite searching the boat thoroughly, the boys drew a blank. There was nothing to eat or drink on board. All they found was a packet of rather mouldy looking biscuits tucked away in a corner of the vessel. Paul pitched these overboard in disgust.

'Pity the canopy blew away,' said Paul a little later, when he had recovered from his shock of not finding any food aboard the little vessel. 'If the sun gets much stronger, we shall get absolutely scorched, to say nothing of being parched.'

Chris nodded grimly. He knew this was the biggest danger facing them now.

For a long time after the storm had died away, they drifted in silence over the smooth glassy waves, the sun beating down on them all the while. It was so hot that Chris felt his normally white skin burning. Paul, who was darker than Chris, began to wonder if he was melting. The boys sat uncomplaining most of the time, not daring to drink the salt water which surrounded them, because Chris remembered the tales he had been told about shipwrecked sailors. Salt water, he told Paul, was very dangerous to drink; it made you thirstier, and people had been known to die through drinking it, because the salt sped up the dehydration process. What might have happened to them before long, no one knows, but just as they were beginning to feel they couldn't last much longer without a drink to cool them against the terrible heat, Paul fancied he could hear waves breaking against rocks.

'Perhaps we are near the shore,' he suggested.

'Either that, or we are about to be wrecked on the rocks,' said Chris gloomily.

'I can hear seagulls, that must mean we are near land,' said Paul excitedly.

'That's probably only your imagination,' Chris commented sourly. He had given up all hope of reaching the shore.

As they drew nearer the sound of breaking water, the boat began to pitch violently. The two friends clung desperately to the sides of the boat, hoping that they weren't going to suffer from the same conditions they had experienced during the storm. By now the blue water, which had surrounded them for the last few hours, had turned to white foam, which lashed the sides of their craft, making it twist and turn in the swell. Up and down rocked the vessel, water slopping over the sides, wetting them, making them feel cold, despite the heat of the strong sun.

'An island!' spluttered Chris as a large wave kicked him in the teeth. 'I think we're going to be all right.'

Crash!

Their vessel had struck a rock. Chris and Paul were pitched into the sea. Desperately they tried to cling to the wreckage, but the bottom of the vessel had been torn out by the violence of the collision. The boat began to sink in the boiling waters. The sky appeared to be wheeling round and round as the waves swept them both off their feet. Chris felt sure that this was the end.

'Ugh!' exclaimed Paul in disgust. He hated the taste of seawater.

'Help!' gasped Chris. He felt himself sink for the second time. A hand yanked him to his feet. It was Paul.

'Thanks!' groaned Chris. He wasn't a good swimmer, but Paul had been school champion for two years running. Paul didn't stop at hauling Chris to his feet. He began to drag him roughly through the shallows, afraid that another wave would come and swamp them both. Eventually, they reached a spot where they both could stand upright, without any fear of sinking again. They looked back, but it was a vain hope. The little craft was by this time upside down and breaking up fast, as the waves pounded it against the rocks.

'Are you all right?'

'I think so,' said Chris between chattering teeth.

'Hold on to me. I think we can make the beach all right.'

Chris did as he was told, and Paul managed to force a passage through the waves, which sometimes reached up to his shoulders. Soon they were standing on the beach, their breath coming in great heaving gasps and their clothes wringing wet.

'Come on! This is no place to stop,' Paul warned.

'Why not?'

'That wave over there, I think it is coming our way!'

Chris glanced in the direction Paul was pointing. He didn't need to be told twice. A huge green wall of water was heading their way. He began to run clumsily after Paul. The great wave caught them both before they could reach higher ground and threw them both over, but by this time the worst was over. They soon picked themselves up and could run further up the beach to a place where the waves could not reach them. Within a few minutes they were lying gasping, but safe upon a warm sand dune, about half-a-mile from where the waves continued to tear apart their boat and worry the jagged rocks.

There were some trees growing further up the beach, and when they had recovered some of their strength, they began to make their way in that direction. Chris collapsed into the shade of one tree, and lay like a stranded pink fish. Then Paul toppled over in a heap and lay still.

Patch Is Captured

'Mr Higgotty?' Stella inquired nervously. She was doing her best to carry out Chris and Paul's instructions by contacting the fat policeman.

'And who might you be?' asked the policeman fixing her with a fierce state.

'My name is Stella and I'm a prisoner of the wizard.'

'Now! Now!' warned the policeman. 'Don't play silly games with me. I won't stand for it. You know there are no such things as wizards.'

'Oh!' Stella gasped. She felt totally confused. Had Chris and Paul really spoken with the policeman? He was acting as if they had never spoken to him at all, it was most strange.

'But you are Mr Higgotty, the policeman, aren't you?'

'That is my name.'

Stella breathed a quick sigh of relief, but her relief was short-lived.

'At least,' continued the policeman. 'I thought I was me, but I am not so sure.'

'Whatever do you mean?' Stella asked uncertainly. Surely the policeman wasn't still suffering from the ill-effects of the spell Zardaka had cast upon him?

'Look!' she said. 'I haven't much time to explain. The two boys, you were after, sent me here to fetch you. You're to come with me now.'

The policeman frowned. 'How do I know I can trust you?'

'Oh dear!' sighed Stella. She took a deep breath. 'I don't suppose anything I say will make the slightest difference to what you believe, but what I am going to tell you is the truth.'

'Go on.'

'The mistake you are making is that you think this garden is the same world that you inhabit.'

Higgotty scratched his head thoughtfully. 'All I did was climb a ladder,' he said.

'And Zardaka changed you into a snake.'

The policeman stared at her in surprise. 'Oh, you know about that?'

'Chris and Paul told me.'

'Who are Chris and Paul?'

It was Stella's turn to stare at the policeman.

'You know,' she said. 'The two boys you were chasing. They were accused of shoplifting. Now do you believe me?'

Higgotty ignored the question. He looked over his shoulder.

'I see the door in the wall has gone,' he said. 'I can't send for reinforcements.'

Stella stamped her foot furiously.

'Oh! Why won't you listen!' she snapped angrily. 'I keep telling you, we cannot leave this garden as easily as we entered it, because we are now in a different world.' She paused to see if her words had any effect. The policeman still looked confused, but Stella could see he was trying hard to understand. 'Come on,' she said more gently.

'I can't explain things out here. You must come with me. The boys have slipped into that forest over there to try and find some way of beating Zardaka at his own game.'

Eventually, they reached Stella's room. Higgotty went over to the window and gazed into the approaching darkness. The forest looked gloomy and foreboding in the twilight. An eerie howling sounded in the distance.

'What on earth was that?' inquired the policeman.

'Wolves,' said Stella casually.

'Wolves!'

'And bears. What do you expect in Canada?'

'Canada! I thought you said this was Zardaka's world?'

'So I did. But I forgot to mention that his house overlooks the world, I mean our world.' Stella went on to explain about the different views from each window in the house and how she had tried to escape.

By now it was completely dark outside. Stella switched on a table lamp, but she did not draw the curtains, or completely close the window.

'So we can listen out for the boys,' she explained. 'Do you feel hungry?'

'Come to think of it, I do.'

Stella clapped her hands and the two mysteriously shrouded figures appeared.

'What in the name of horror are they supposed to be?' exclaimed the policeman.

Stella laughed. 'They are harmless enough. You'll get used to them in time. They are Zardaka's servants.'

'What is your wish?' asked one of the figures.

'I want you to bring us food,' commanded Stella.

The figures bowed and disappeared. A few minutes later they reappeared and a meal was set upon a white cloth on a low table.

'Come on!' Let's eat!' Stella invited.

For a long time there was silence.

'Gosh!' Mr Higgotty gasped, swallowing a last mouthful. 'That was some meal.'

'Yes, they keep me well fed, even though I'm a prisoner.'

Higgotty immediately lost his momentary gaiety and at once resumed his more ponderous manner. 'I am forgetting myself,' he apologised. 'Pardon me, Miss.'

'All I want to do,' Stella said sadly, 'is to go home.'

The policeman stared at her for a few moments thoughtfully.

'Here!' he exclaimed. 'I've got something which may interest you.' He fished into the breast pocket of his tunic and brought out a slightly tattered folded newspaper cutting. Breathing heavily, he unfolded it for her.

'This must be you,' he said jabbing a stumpy finger at a faded photograph. Stella took the yellowed clipping from the policeman.

'Yes,' she said slowly. 'That's me.'

'I only kept the cutting out of curiosity,' Mr Higgotty explained. 'I had a funny feeling that I might come across you eventually. You see,' the policeman added half-apologetically, 'where you used to live used to be part of my beat.'

'How do you mean?' Stella frowned.

'I know White Meadows, the place you disappeared well, and I thought I might succeed in finding some clue, when others had failed.'

'Well, it was nice of you to keep looking, when I suppose everyone else had given up,' Stella said gratefully. The newspaper was dated the previous May:

Stella Holmes of 42 Station Road, Westcutting-on-Sea disappeared mysteriously yesterday whilst playing with her friends. Playmate Dawn Jennings of Wood Avenue said that she had been playing with Stella shortly before her disappearance. It is alleged that a black kitten wandered up to them in White Meadows, which is quite close to the estate where Stella lives. Somehow the missing girl became separated from her friends when she ran after the kitten. Dawn said that the last she saw of Stella was when her friend ran into the wood, which borders White Meadows and the town reservoir. When Stella failed to return from the wood, the other children searched for her, but were unable to find her, even though her footprints were still showing in the soft mud. Somewhere in the centre of the wood the footprints mysteriously ceased. Police tracker dogs also drew a blank, but a police spokesman said last night that they do not suspect foul play. Stella attends Viscount Comprehensive School. Her headmaster and form teacher both confirmed that she always appeared to be happy there.

A photograph, not very flattering, completed the article, with Stella, in school uniform, smiling rather uncertainly at the camera. Silently she handed the cutting back to the policeman. 'I'd clean forgot about it until now,' said Higgotty, puzzlement all over his honest face. At least I'll be able to please my Inspector, when we get back, by handing you over to your parents.' He got up from his seat and began to walk around the room examining the ornaments for the second time, muttering to himself as he did so. Like Chris and Paul, he had begun to experience the same uneasy bewilderment that they had felt on first entering the room.

Behind a velvet curtain Patch's green eyes flickered wickedly. His master would be pleased when he heard of Patch's discovery of the whereabouts of the policeman. And if he waited a little longer, he might even find out what had happened to the boys. He settled down more comfortably behind the curtain, listening to every word which was spoken between Stella and the policeman.

'The other rooms,' Higgotty was saying. 'You haven't shown me those yet.'

Stella fingered the gold medallion she wore about her neck.

'The other rooms won't help,' she said.

'All right then. Think hard. What is the most unusual feature about this house and garden, miss?'

'Maybe,' she said slowly, 'the fountain you saw in the centre of the lawn holds some clue. Everything seems to happen there. If you remember me telling you, Zardaka appeared out of a rainbow. That's how Paul and Chris saw him for the first time.'

'This rainbow, how is it important to Zardaka?' asked Higgotty.

'I think it is some kind of force,' Stella said. 'It may be the key to everything.'

95

In his effort to hear every word that was being spoken, Patch moved forward. There was a slight rustle of fabric.

'I've never looked at the fountain properly,' Stella confessed. 'However, I did notice a blue bird there once.'

'Oh?' asked the policeman curiously.

'Yes. The bird was not much bigger than a robin. And you know, I had the strangest feeling it wanted to talk to me. Silly wasn't I?'

Higgotty didn't answer. Stella stared at him in surprise. The policeman was watching the curtains with a strange look on his face.

'What on earth is it?' Stella asked in a frightened voice. For one awful moment, she wondered if the wizard might have returned. Her heart leapt into her throat, and she felt as if she were about to choke with terror. Higgotty put a restraining finger to his lip. Despite his large bulk, he moved quickly across the room and pounced on something black and furry, with a white spot over one eye, hidden behind the red velvet curtains.

'Well! Well! What have we got here?' inquired Higgotty.

'Patch! Spying and prying as usual!' Stella exclaimed.

Relief that it wasn't the wizard showed in her voice. And sure enough, it was Patch, spitting and yowling, desperately scratching and struggling in the strong grip of the policeman.

'Some cat!' marvelled the brave Higgotty, protecting himself as best as he could from the cruel claws.

'And I wonder what you were doing behind that curtain?'

'Oh, please don't hurt him!' screamed Stella in terror. 'He is always like that, spying and telling tales to Zardaka about me. It is his nature; Patch doesn't know any better. I feel quite sure that he didn't really mean any harm.'

'And I am quite sure,' said the policeman grimly. 'What's your name, my lad? Come on now, or I shall have to find some way of loosening your tongue.' PC Higgotty wouldn't have hurt a fly, but Patch wasn't to know that. He was used to people carrying out their threats.

'P-p-please, mm-mmy n-name is P-P-Patch,' stammered the cat.

'That's a funny name to have,' said the policeman.

'I m-meant, P-Patch,' gasped the cat.

'And you really can talk, or am I dreaming?'

'Yes. B-but I c-could s-speak mm-much b-better, if you loosened your g-grip a little. Y-you are m-making it very d-difficult for me to b-breath at all!'

'And if I do that, will you try to escape?'

'No—oh no!'

'Very well, but as a precaution, because I don't fully trust you, I will do this!' Before Patch fully realised what was happening, Higgotty had handcuffed him.

'How on earth did you know Patch was behind the curtain?' Stella asked.

'I could see the curtains moving from time to time, that's why I took several walks around the room. I knew eventually our little friend would over reach himself and give the game away.'

Stella stared at Mr Higgotty in admiration. For the first time, she realised that he was a much better constable than either Chris or Paul had given him credit.

'Poor Patch isn't such a good spy after all,' she observed. 'What are we going to do with him now?'

'He'll just have to come with us to that fountain. We can't leave him here. If we do, he'll blab everything he's overheard to his master.'

'What a nuisance!' Stella exclaimed.

'I-I promise n-not to m-m-make a sound!' gasped Patch. 'P-please l-let m-me go!'

'Come along!' ordered Higgotty. 'We've wasted enough time as it is.'

Stella led the way, creeping along the deserted corridors of the house, keeping well to the shadows, with Mr Higgotty following, holding Patch firmly by the scruff of his neck. Everything was dark and silent after the mysterious tinkling of the chandeliers and the strange patterned lights which filled the wizard's home. Because everything looked so dark and creepy, Stella suggested they waited for a few moments, until their eyes grew more accustomed to the night. As they waited, an owl hooted eerily to the left, making them jump and sending shivers up their spines.

'Mista, the wizard's owl!' Stella breathed softly into Higgotty's ear. Then the moon broke from its coverings of cloud, illuminating the garden with soft silvery light. Leaves stood out, black and hard, like cardboard cut outs, etched into sharp relief. Flowers glowed mysteriously, hovering like strange white moths above their heads. Stella felt sure that everything appeared unnatural because of the magic she felt in the cool night air. No earthly moon, for example, would behave quite as this one did.

'Come on!' hissed Higgotty impatiently. 'This is no time to stand gawping. Anyone would think you'd never seen the moon before. We must make a run for it, Miss. Mista will spot us soon enough, if we stand in the light.'

Stella knew that the policeman was right. With an effort, she shook herself free of her trance. Between them they dragged the unwilling Patch along the ghostly grass walks. Ever afraid of being spotted by the sharp-eyed Mista, they did their best to keep to the shadows. Heavy flowers spilled their overpowering scent into their hot faces, as they stumbled between the almost luminous tall shrubs which lined the walks. Then to her horror, Stella heard the flap of wings.

'Down!' she commanded. They were just in time to escape detection. From their hiding place beneath one of the bushes, they saw a huge bat-like shape gliding between the trees. Moonlight glistened on the wings like quicksilver against the indigo sky.

Instantly Higgotty closed his great right hand over the mouth of the cat, so that the poor creature was almost suffocated. Higgotty was determined to take no chances and was afraid that somehow Patch would make a signal to the owl.

Mista alighted on the branch of a tree and waited, his big yellow eyes staring unwinkingly at the landscape. He knew that something or someone was in the garden, his senses told him that, but where?

Higgotty became impatient with the long wait. He knew that it wouldn't be long before they were discovered. Therefore, he had to do something. Very carefully he eased a large stone out of the soft subsoil beneath the bush, underneath which they were hiding. He showed it to Stella and smiled. She nodded to show her approval. The policeman peered through a tiny gap in the foliage at the owl, trying to make up his mind where he should throw his missile. Then he drew back his arm, with well-practised aim from his cricketing days, and sent the stone whirling across the garden. There was a resounding crash as the stone hit something solid, and then a deafening noise of breaking glass. Mista instantly spread his wings and flew off to investigate.

'Crumbs! I wasn't expecting a racket as that!' exclaimed the policeman. 'Quick! There is no time to lose! To the fountain! He grasped Stella by the arm and hauled her to her feet. Together they broke into a stumbling run, dragging the unfortunate Patch with them. A few minutes later they were standing beside the fountain.

'What now?' Higgotty inquired.

'What do you mean?'

'How is this fountain of yours going to help us?'

'I don't know!' Stella wailed.

PC Higgotty took a deep breath.

'Pull yourself together!' he urged. 'Think!'

Stella couldn't. She shook her head desperately.

'You'll have to think of something soon. Mista will be back on our trail when he finds out it was only some old greenhouse I've broken.'

Stella looked around, desperately trying to remember what Chris had told her about the fountain. She watched the stone dolphins spurting water through their mouths into the crown shaped bowl of the fountain. Tears of mortification began to run down her face. What a fool she had been! Then she began to stare at the fountain in disbelief. A bird, no larger than a robin, with bright blue feathers, a yellow beak and matching legs, stood on the rim of the crown shaped fountain. Even as Stella looked, the bird winked its beady black eyes at her and a bubbling song gushed from its throbbing throat. It was as if the bird wanted to speak to her, but couldn't quite.

'I think we are supposed to follow the bird,' said Higgotty.

'But where?' asked Stella, looking around in puzzlement.

'You're not going to believe this,' replied Higgotty with a smile. 'Into the fountain!'

'What on earth for?' Stella demanded crossly. 'Really! Is this some kind of joke, if it is I don't find it very funny!'

'Neither do I,' said the policeman grimly. 'But I can assure you, that is what the bird wants us to do.'

'That fountain looks very deep,' Stella observed doubtfully. 'Won't we drown?'

'We might.'

'Then what is the point?'

'Mista. He's right behind us, if you haven't forgotten.'

Stella shook her head. 'I don't like water much,' she confessed.

'Ugh! Ugh!' gurgled Patch from behind his gag.

'Oh! The poor thing! I believe he wants to tell us something. Perhaps you'd better untie his gag.'

'Then he'll shout for help. No, Miss. He's only trying to say that he doesn't like water; in fact, I never met a cat that did.'

'Don't be horrid!' protested Stella. 'He'll choke if you don't do something. Besides, Mista is not about at the moment. Please take the gag off.'

Rather unwillingly, Higgotty did as Stella requested. Patch, minus the gag, glared wickedly at both, but did not attempt to say anything. He was too afraid of the policeman to speak.

'What do we do now?' Stella asked.

'Jump into the fountain, just as the bird asks. This is a very strange garden, but I feel something wonderful will happen.'

'Yes, we'll all get wet!' muttered Patch.

'Hold your tongue!' commanded the policeman. 'No one asked for your opinion.'

'I can't swim,' Stella admitted.

The policeman looked at her in astonishment.

'How old are you?' he asked.

'Twelve.'

'Twelve!' repeated Higgotty in astonishment.

'There is nothing particularly wonderful about that. I'm fourteen and I can't swim either,' said Patch in a surly voice.

'Will you be quiet!' snapped the policeman sternly.

'I'm not going in that fountain,' Patch protested.

'You must do as we do, and that is final.'

'But I've got a weak chest. Everyone knows that. You don't know how bad water is.'

'Silence!' hissed Stella. 'Do you think we want to know your entire medical history?'

Patch shut up.

The bird began to speak to them again. Although it could only speak to them in its own language, a series of trills and muted notes, it was quite clear from its actions what it wanted them to do. The bird half-beckoned to them with its wings, as if willing them to follow it, then dived into the spray of the fountain. Each time the bird disappeared into the spray, Stella felt sure it would never again reappear, but it did. Once the bird alighted on the fountain's rim, impatiently shrilling out its urgent song, shaking tiny droplets of water into the air, so that they shone like transparent crystals. Stella watched the spots of water glistening like molten beads in the moonlight, before they shattered themselves into fragments against the foaming water. The bird winked its jet-black eyes at them and nodded its head, before pouring out another plaintive song.

'You see!' Higgotty explained. 'We must follow the bird.'

'Well,' said Stella reluctantly. 'If that is what we must do, then there is no point in hanging around, is there?'

The policeman clapped her on the back.

'That's the spirit, Miss!' he said.

Inwardly, Stella was trembling with fear as she gazed into the clearness of the water. How deep the water stood in the fountain bowl, there was no way of telling. As she stood on the rim of the fountain, she tried to summon up all her courage to jump. She watched the bubbling water for a moment. What was that? Surely she was mistaken. No, there it went again. Stella leaned forward, as far as she dared. There was something flashing, appearing at certain intervals in the clear depths. She rubbed her eyes fiercely, refusing to believe that she had seen anything, then looked again. Could it have been a fish? Even as she wondered, the rainbow flash of light appeared again. Stella gripped the edge of the fountain so tightly, her knuckles went white with the strain.

'Do you see what I see?' she asked in a strangled voice. 'A flash of light, rather like a rainbow, but, oh! so much brighter.'

PC Higgotty shook his head doubtfully. 'Perhaps it is the reflection of the moon or stars,' he suggested. 'I am sure that it is nothing to worry about.' He looked over his shoulder apprehensively.

'You'd better hurry, miss,' he urged. 'I don't know when Mista will reappear, but it can't be long now.'

Stella took a long breath, then she nodded slowly. She held on to the policeman's hand. All three stood on the rim of the fountain. The bird flew above their heads, excited at the fact that they were about to do as it asked. Higgotty didn't seem at all concerned about jumping into the cauldron, but Patch was shaking with terror. He was so frightened, that for once, he had nothing to say! As for Stella, well, she was having second thoughts over jumping into the fountain, despite her resolve to be brave. In fact, she would have given almost anything she owned if she could have turned back at that moment, but she knew that this was impossible. Then something awful happened. There was a clap of wings as Mista the Owl launched himself at them without warning. Mista had completed his investigations of the broken greenhouse and had concluded that he had been tricked. His long swoop over the shadowy garden ended with a great tearing sound as his talons ripped open a great gaping hole in the back of PC Higgotty's tunic. The policeman half-turned to meet his attacker, but it was a vain attempt. Within seconds of the attack, he had overbalanced and fallen into the fountain, carrying Patch with him. Poor Patch gave a howl of fear as he hit the water. Helplessly, Stella watched the cat spitting and scratching desperately, before it was carried under the foaming torrent. As for Higgotty, one minute he was swimming strongly against the current, and the next moment, he had been caught up in a great whirlpool. Stella gave a terrible scream as he was sucked down into the vortex. She was alone, left to face Mista by herself. The great wings of the owl cast a shadow across her face as a pair of expressionless yellow eyes bored into hers. Desperately she ducked, but even as she did so, Stella felt a violent blow against her face. Screaming with terror she toppled slowly backwards into the water. Gasping and spluttering she surfaced quickly. Water ran up her nose, making her cough and splutter. She tried breathing through her mouth, but instead swallowed a mouthful of water. A strange lassitude seemed to be spreading through her body, so that she lost her will and strength to struggle against her fate. At first Stella tried to fight this feeling, especially when she felt herself sinking, but each time she struggled against the water, something happened to her mind, so that she found herself becoming progressively weaker. Her golden hair snaked about her, weightless and free, but the black velvet dress continued to drag her down. Down she went, twisting slightly as the invisible currents caught her. There was a slight 'pop' of trailing bubbles as Stella disappeared into the depths of the water.

Mista watched curiously. He sat motionless on the rim of the fountain, watching the girl's thrashing movements grow increasingly feeble. Now, only a trail of silvery bubbles marked her departure from Zardaka's world. He was satisfied. Two destroyed, without much difficulty on his part. A pity about the cat, but that couldn't be helped. It was no concern of Mista's that Patch had been destroyed along with Zardaka's enemies. Mista yawned and then gave a cruel chuckle. He had never liked cats very much. Nasty creepy things, with their long tails swishing from side to side, to say nothing of their cruel claws. No, it was a good thing the cat was gone.

Finally, a mysterious thing happened. A bright rainbow suddenly began to materialise above the fountain. The rainbow grew brighter and brighter, until it was almost as bright as the sun. Mista hastily drew back, and flew into the darker reaches of the garden, as far as he could from the strong light. It wasn't that Mista was frightened, quite the opposite; but like all owls, he hated brightness.

Through the Rainbow

A strange whispering seemed to fill Stella's head. She moaned softly, but kept her eyes firmly closed against the bright light which threatened to break into her dark tranquil world. The whispering increased in its intensity.

'Oh blow! What do you want now?' Stella grumbled crossly.

'I was having a lovely dream and you had to come along and spoil it.' She opened her eyes a fraction, but the bright light made her shut them tight again. Abruptly the whispering stopped. Gingerly Stella tried to see again. She peeped through the curtain of her long eyelashes, trying to make out where she was. To her surprise, she was lying in a green sunlit meadow. A rainbow was shining above her head, a great multi-coloured arc of light, dazzling in its brilliance. Stella hid her face in her hands. When she ventured to peep out again, the rainbow had vanished.

Stella got to her feet, she felt a little dizzy, but otherwise she felt all right. A skylark was twittering high in the azure sky and pretty butterflies were dancing on zoned wings above the brightly coloured flowers, but she could see no sign of Patch or the policeman. She inspected her clothes, which were dry and comfortable, although they should have still been wet from her jump in the fountain. Her mind had gone blank, blotting out certain details from the past. She screwed her face into a fierce frown of concentration. Surely she could remember what had happened to her? Slowly, the image of Mista emerged from her subconscious. It was an ugly memory, not very pleasant to recall at all. She remembered him knocking her into the water, her feeble thrashing, and then a period of nothing. Had she drowned? Was this the after-life? Stella thought not. For one thing, she did not really feel very much different from usual, except she half-suspected she had been asleep for a very long time. It had been night when she had fallen into the fountain, now it was day and the sun was high in the sky, so something very strange had occurred whilst she had been asleep. But where was Higgotty?

Stella stared about her curiously. Except for the insects droning away in the distance, and the skylark singing high above her, she was alone. For some reason, she didn't really feel at all frightened, even though she had no idea where she was, or what she was doing in that meadow. A gentle breeze stirred the summer flowers, so that they swayed their heads to the rustling sound made by the long grass stems as they brushed against one another. Bewildered, Stella continued to stare about her for quite some time, marvelling at the blueness of the sky, the bright colours of the flowers and butterflies, as they tripped from bloom to bloom. Then she became aware of the strength of the sun. Stella wished she'd worn one of the summer frocks, which the wizard had provided for her, instead of this black velvet dress, with its impractical lace collar and sleeves. She tossed her fair hair back and wondered what she ought to do next. Perhaps there were some shady trees on the other side of the meadow? But which side, and what direction would be best? The meadow sloped slightly, so Stella decided it would be best to walk downhill. It would be less tiring and not so hot. Hesitantly, Stella began to walk. Where the breeze stirred the long grass, the meadow appeared to move, just as if it were alive. The grass stems rattled a harsh song, which ran in a circular direction around the field, like some mysterious whispered litany, making its way round an empty church. Stella felt a little nervous, but not afraid, because she had begun to believe that she was out of the wizard's world. Somehow, she knew she was free at last.

Once she had started walking, Stella began to feel more cheerful; she even began to sing snatches of song to herself, something she had not done during the long days of her captivity. It took her about half-an-hour to reach the edge of the meadow. To her surprise, there wasn't a hedge dividing the field from the road, but a ditch. Slimy-green water had seeped through the earth banks during the winter months. Although it was now summer, the water remained, very still and stagnant, and very unpleasant.

'Pooh!' Stella exclaimed in disgust, wrinkling up her nose at the stench. 'I don't fancy wading through that. I wonder if there is some way round?'

So she walked for some time beside the ditch until she came to a bridge. It wasn't much of a bridge, just a few planks nailed together, but strong enough to allow the farmer, who owned the field, to get his horse and cart across. Carefully, Stella stepped across the bridge. On the other side of the bridge was a rutted track. If one were feeling charitable, it might have been described as a road. In the distance, there were trees growing. Stella decided to walk towards them. It was still very hot and before long she felt the perspiration running down her neck. She picked up a large leaf which she found growing beside the track and began to fan herself. Stella felt very uncomfortable walking in the hot sunshine. Her foot began to hurt. She stopped to rest and found a stone had worked itself into her shoe, causing the heel to blister slightly. Sitting on the grass beside the track, Stella had another shock, her silver shoes had changed to gold! She couldn't believe this for a moment, so she rubbed her shoes with her handkerchief. Laughing with relief, Stella found that the dust from the road had caused the change in appearance. She brushed the shoes carefully and then wearily resumed her journey. After a long time, she reached the shelter of the trees. Flopping exhaustedly, she leaned against the rough bark of an oak, breathing in the fresh air, the coolness of the trees helping her revive her shattered senses.

It was some time before she had recovered sufficiently to look about her. The trees stretched back further than she had expected. Stella felt curious, despite her tiredness from the heat. From a secret pocket, she extracted a small phial of perfume. If Paul had been observing this, he would have shaken his head in disgust, because it was the same perfume which he and Chris had noticed, just before discovering the secret room in which Stella had been found sleeping. Paul was not there, however, to voice his disapproval, so Stella dabbed a little perfume on her face and behind her ears, in imitation of her older sister Cassandra. Her mother would have been very cross, no doubt, if she had been there! Refreshed, Stella began to look cautiously about her. From time to time she had thought she'd heard voices, but that might well be her imagination. She peeped behind the oak tree, but saw nothing, so she began to move forward carefully, step by step. The voices sounded again and then faded. Could she be mistaken? Was it her imagination, or was it something else, something more sinister? Stella couldn't decide, so she walked forward, the trees growing darker and darker about her, until she could hardly see at all. Nervously she looked over her shoulder. Reassuringly the sun shone as golden as before, twinkling comfortably, wrapped in its lacy cocoon of leaves and branches. Stella began to feel more confident. After all, if anything did go wrong, she could always go back. She started forward again.

'Ugh!' Stella exclaimed. The firm ground beneath her feet had given way to mud, red clay, soft and sticky, clinging like toffee to the soles of her silver shoes. Wet leaves slapped her face, and all about her the undergrowth dripped water. Stella looked curiously at the change which had taken place about her. Then she started with surprise.

'It can't be!' she whispered aloud. 'I—I recognise this wood!' There was no doubt about it; she had reached the identical spot where the black kitten she had been chasing had turned into Zardaka. She was free at last! Stella almost danced for joy; she was so delighted to be out of the wizard's clutches; then she froze in her tracks, her joy turning to doubt and despair. Who would belief her story when she reached home? She had no one to back up her story, not even PC Higgotty.

'Yes, Stella,' her father would say. 'We know you stayed with a wicked wizard, but don't you think it is time you stopped pretending and told us what really happened? Your mother and I have been worried sick over you. We've had the police and everyone out looking for you.

111

Now tell me the truth, where have you been?' And her mother would cry and say she was a naughty girl to run off like that and not tell anyone where she was. Stella couldn't face a scene like that. What on earth was she going to do? What could she tell everyone?

A familiar looking path led Stella out of the gloomy patch of woodland into White Meadows. When she reached the edge of the wood she stopped, because the murmur of voices had started up again. Cautiously Stella peered out between the wet leaves of a large bush. Five or six children were running about and chasing a ball. They were boys, but there was a girl, looking rather bored, standing apart from them watching. Stella recognised the girl as her friend Dawn Jennings, the same girl who had described Stella's disappearance to the reporter from the *Westcutting Gazette*. Stella wondered if she could catch Dawn's attention without the other children seeing her. Perhaps Dawn would be able to help her think up a convincing explanation to tell her parents? Stella waited a long time watching. There was a cold wind gusting across the meadow, and she shivered, wishing she'd appreciated the warm sun on the other side of the wood. The black velvet dress was not warm enough. Summer in Britain meant nothing when it came to normal temperatures. Stella couldn't help thinking wistfully back to the sunny meadow, with the butterflies and skylark singing overhead in that gorgeous blue sky. Here in White Meadows, grey clouds scudded across a depressing landscape of saturated leaves and tired looking grass. Stella felt the dampness of an English summer seeping into her bones. Shifting her freezing feet, she felt like an alien from another planet as she gazed across the meadow to the housing estate on which she lived.

Stella was still wondering what to do when a loud shout startled her. The football the children were playing with had been kicked with considerable force in her direction. She watched it coming flying towards her, carelessly kicked out of reach by one of the players. Stella shrank back, hoping that no one would discover her.

'I'll get it!' she heard one of the children cry.

Stella peered between the leaves as she heard running footsteps. A girl came puffing and panting towards her. To Stella's great relief, it was her best friend, Dawn Jennings. The football had rolled into a gap between the bush Stella was hiding behind and a cluster of small sycamore trees.

'Stella Holmes! Is it really you?'

Stella put her finger to her lips.

'Ssh! I don't want anyone to know I'm here.'

Dawn nodded understandingly.

'Come back, when you've got rid of the ball, I have something to tell you. Don't let the others know I'm here.'

Obligingly Dawn left her and brought the ball back to the other children. They thanked her and resumed their game, never guessing for one moment that Dawn had been talking to Stella. Dawn pretended to watch the game for a few minutes and then gradually, in the most casual way she could muster, began to move back to the place where she had seen Stella.

'Where on earth have you been?' Dawn asked crossly. 'You can't imagine how much trouble you've caused. Everyone has been looking for you. You must be mad to stay in this wood.' She shivered. 'I bet it must be cold staying here.'

'I didn't stay in the wood!' Stella hissed indignantly. 'And before you go on at me, you might at least listen to my side of the story.'

Dawn muttered something rude under her breath.

'What happened then?' she asked ungraciously. 'And why all this secrecy? Surely it doesn't matter if those kids see you or not?'

'I'm not so sure about that,' Stella said. 'Come here, out of sight of everyone, and I'll tell you what happened to me.'

Dubiously Dawn followed Stella into the wood. She half-wondered if her friends had gone mad, she was acting so strangely. Why had her friend disappeared suddenly like that? If it was a joke, she was going to get very cross with Stella.

'Let me borrow your coat for a moment,' Stella begged. 'I'm freezing with cold.'

'I'm not surprised, staying out here for so long. And why are you wearing those ridiculous clothes and those funny shoes?' Dawn sounded most disapproving. Stella's heart sank. If her friend refused to help her, then who would?

'I can't understand why you are behaving as you are,' Dawn continued. 'Why don't you go home, like any normal person? Your parents won't be angry with you forever, you know. Or is it that you want me to come with you, to help tell them what happened?'

'No, it isn't quite like that, Dawn,' Stella tried to explain. Her friend looked blankly at her. 'Oh dear! Perhaps I'd better tell you the whole story.'

'From beginning to end,' said Stella grimly. 'And don't leave anything out, because I want to hear it all.'

Stella sighed. 'Here, put my coat on for a bit,' Dawn offered.

'Oh, that is so much better!' Stella said, snuggling down into her friend's warm coat.

'Now tell me the story!'

And that's just what Stella did.

'I suppose you don't believe me,' she said when she had completed telling Dawn every detail of her escape back into White Meadows.

'Well you must admit, it is fantastic, but...'

'But what?' Stella asked anxiously, as her friend paused to gather her thoughts.

'I really don't know what to say,' Dawn confessed.

'I half expected you to say that,' Stella said dolefully. 'Now you begin to understand my problem and how I feel about my parents hearing such a story. They won't believe me any more than you do.'

'Well, Stella, you must admit it is a fantastic story,' Dawn admonished.

'I knew you wouldn't believe me,' Stella said sadly.

'I didn't say that. I only said it was fantastic. That's not quite the same thing you know.' Stella frowned at Dawn. She felt her friend did not believe her. What on earth was she going to do? 'I know!' Dawn exclaimed brightly. 'Why don't you show me this other world?' she suggested.

Stella's face brightened.

'After all,' Dawn reasoned. 'If you could walk out of that world into this one, you should be able to find your way back. You said yourself, it was easier to enter this wizard's world than to try and escape from it.'

'We could try,' Stella agreed. 'After all, I would like to know what happened to Mr Higgotty and the others. Do you want your coat back yet?'

'No. I can keep myself warm walking. Your sunny day in the other world should warm me up.'

Stella gave Dawn a suspicious look. She thought Dawn was making fun of her, but her friend had started striding ahead, eager to find the hidden world. Although Stella's story sounded odd, Dawn was prepared to believe her. For one thing, she had read of stranger things happening in some of her father's books, and for another, she had never known Stella tell lies, whether it be at school or home.

'We must be near the entry to your world by now; if we go any further, we'll reach the reservoir,' Dawn said after half-an-hour of searching.

'I'm not sure if we've come far enough yet,' Stella replied uncertainly. Ten minutes later, she had to admit defeat.

'Oh dear!' she exclaimed tearfully. 'I don't know what has happened.' She began to look all around, very carefully, trying to find the opening to the sunny country she had so recently left. 'I must have dreamed it,' she muttered to herself. But in her heart, she knew that this was simply not true. For one thing, she still wore the strange silver slippers upon her feet and the black velvet dress, together with the gold medallion and ring. Maybe they could help her? But how? Eventually, Dawn helped her to find her footprints and they followed them as far as they could.

Dawn was puzzled. 'It is just like the time you disappeared,' she said. 'You say the hard ground turned to mud?'

'That's right. It was very sticky. I could hardly walk.'

'And then what?'

'I found the path leading to where you were watching those boys playing football.'

Dawn looked a little uncomfortable. 'I was bored,' she explained. 'There hasn't been much for me to do on my own since you disappeared.'

'I'm sorry,' Stella apologised.

'Well, it doesn't look as if we are going to find the entry to your world. Have you any more ideas before we pack it in?'

Stella thought carefully.

'The policeman told me something about an entrance into Zardaka's world through the wall in Back Lane.'

Dawn clapped her hands. 'That's it!' she exclaimed. 'Why don't we go there?' Then she paused. 'Only, I think you should go home first, so that your parents at least know you are all right.'

'I could go to your house first. Maybe you and your father would back my story,' Stella suggested. If she could convince Dawn's father that she was speaking the truth, her parents would have no option but to believe her story.

'My father would be very interested to hear what happened to you,' Dawn agreed. 'That garden may turn out to be a perfectly ordinary garden, but I doubt it. Father was saying only the other night that several unexplained incidents have occurred in Back Lane. No one is able to prove anything, but he had an idea that the storm had some connection with your disappearance.'

'Yes, I heard all about the storm,' Stella said. 'That was the storm which Zardaka caused, so that he could frighten all those people away from his garden. It was the day Mr Higgotty the policeman disappeared, you remember? I told you how Chris and Paul saw him turned into a snake. I also heard the story from his own lips.' Stella had a sudden thought. 'Did anyone say anything about a policeman disappearing?'

Dawn shook her head. 'Not as far as I know. All I do know is that my father said someone ought to investigate all those odd things happening in the garden next to Back Lane.'

'So people are suspicious!' Stella exclaimed with satisfaction.

'Yes. And now, if you're ready to go, we'll go and see my father.'

'What about Chris and Paul and Mr Higgotty?'

'They'll just have to look after themselves for the time being. Maybe my father will have some suggestions.'

'Do you think your father will believe me?'

'I believe you.'

This startled Stella, because up to now she had wondered if Dawn was merely humouring her.

'How do you know I'm telling the truth?' she asked.

'You wouldn't have appeared in the wood dressed as you are, unless something very peculiar had happened to you. I'm sure my father will also believe you are telling the truth.'

Stella looked down at her dress and the silver slippers, now caked with a generous helping of red clay, and she couldn't help smiling.

'Come on!' commanded Dawn. 'Let's go. Besides, I'm getting cold.'

Obligingly Stella gave Dawn her coat back.

In the Desert

The mid-day sun was a molten ball of fire in the brass coloured sky. So powerful was the force of the Arabian sun which beat down upon the ochre sands, some have said it was possible to fry an egg on top of one of the flat rocks which appeared at intervals, breaking the monotony of the stark landscape. But there was no one in this desert remotely interesting in frying eggs, least of all the man who could be seen staggering between the dunes which shimmered in the heat haze, reducing visibility to a fraction of what it might have been. The man was trying to follow an almost indistinguishable trail between thorn bushes, gleaming white bones and mysterious ruins. The bones marked an old camel route, which had been used for thousands of years, before being abandoned; the ruins had belonged to an ancient empire, which had exhausted for a few centuries, before crumbling back into dust. What happened to the inhabitants of this great city no one knows, nor is it engraved on the stone tables, which archaeologists excavated and preserved. Perhaps everyone died, along with the vineyards which used to cover this desolate spot, before it turned to desert and the rivers, which had fed the great empire, had finally evaporated, leaving only a scattered population of nomads to carry on the memory of what had once been a great nation. Nor is there anyone left to relate the stories of the hanging gardens, or the family pets, or tell of horses and carts, which used to throng the busy streets. In those days, silversmiths, goldsmiths and jewellers rubbed shoulders with other tradesmen. How mighty were the fallen, when all that remained were a few broken cookery pots?

Our lost traveller was not to know that he was passing over the site of a great city-state; the odds are, he wouldn't have cared less if someone had pointed out to him the frightful significance of these ruins. The man had more important things on his mind; he was trying to survive. His lips were cracked from the heat, and his tongue had swollen, so that he could scarcely swallow. Sensibly, some hours before, he had placed a small pebble in his mouth, and he sucked on this from time to time to try and alleviate his dryness. Even so, he knew unless he found water soon, he would die. That was the law of the desert. As if to remind him of this fact, vultures circled high above, confident that before many more hours had passed, they would be feasting on his flesh.

Just in case you haven't guessed by now who this man was, stumbling about, cursing the flies, the heat and sand, when he should have been conserving his strength, it was none other than our old friend Police Constable Higgotty. But what a change had taken place, for Chris, Paul and Stella would have scarcely recognised this ragged individual, with his wild eyes, unshaven face, brick-red complexion and confusion of uncombed hair. The policeman drew the remains of a red checked handkerchief from his pocket, intending to mop his brow, but to his surprise, his face was dry! There was no perspiration to wipe. Then he realised the truth; the desert is such a hot and arid place that as soon as moisture passes through the pores in the skin it evaporates, and if this process continues indefinitely, the unfortunate traveller becomes dehydrated and finally dies. The human body, being ninety per cent water, needs constant replenishment.

How had Higgotty ended up in this terrible place? He was not sure himself; all he remembered was that awful moment when Mista the Owl had launched his attack. Higgotty's tunic had been ruined in the resulting fight, torn in two by a great slash from the Owl's claws, then the policeman had tumbled into the water, together with Patch, the wizard's cat. The rest of Higgotty's memory was confused; the only clear thought he could extract, without too much difficulty, was the feeling that he had been floating in space, riding on a rainbow, which had somehow looped itself around the earth. The brilliant prism of colours from the rainbow had filled his heart with joy as he floated high above the earth. He had not been conscious of time or direction as he hung suspended above the world. Through a hazy mist he had seen the desert taken shape, stretching itself like a yellow lizard beneath the indigo sky, its flickering tongue touching the white capped mountains, before slithering away, almost shying away, just before it met the emerald forests. A distant sea lapped the shore of his dream, its azure waters mingling with the sky, so that Higgotty could not tell where the one ended and the other began. Then everything became confused. Higgotty had felt like a leaf caught in a gale. Leaping images had crowded in upon his brain, images which pressed against his imagination, overlapping in their haste with reality, causing a sequence of unrelated thoughts. When Higgotty became himself again, all he could see was this awful place, hot and dusty, with no food or water to sustain him. Only the shimmering silence and the flies were there to keep him company, until the vultures arrived. Now they hovered high above his head. Higgotty felt a shiver run down his back. What was he to do now? He had lost track of time. He shook his pocket watch angrily. Blasted thing! It had never gone since the moment he had entered Zardaka's garden. There it was, stopped permanently at ten o'clock. What on earth could be wrong with it? Higgotty scratched his head in bewilderment, and trudged on. A mirage of water danced before his eyes. He closed his eyes tightly to block out the illusion, and as he did, his stumbling feet caught against an obstruction. He felt himself falling. Thump! All the breath was knocked out of his body when he hit the ground. For a long time the policeman lay winded on the sand, breathing the hot gritty air, whilst the vultures circled curiously, swooping increasingly lower, trying to find out whether their intended victim was dead yet.

Getting to his feet, Higgotty looked about him. To his surprise he had wandered right into the centre of the ruined city. There wasn't much left of the city, a few pillars standing here and there, like accusing fingers pointing at the sky; other pillars had fallen, and the forces of time and numerous sandstorms had caused severe weathering. The policeman shaded his eyes; he could make out one or two walls, which must have belonged to one of the many temples, or perhaps to a house, or sumptuous villa. A few thorn bushes had managed to eke out a precarious existence for themselves. Higgotty licked his dry lips and studied the bushes thoughtfully. An idea had struck him. Perhaps there was water somewhere round here? Those bushes were managing to survive and it seemed possible that when the city had been in existence, there must have been a plentiful water supply at one time, otherwise why should the ancients build such an elaborate civilization in such a desolate spot? He scratched his head with puzzlement written all over his face. It was difficult to believe that people had once lived here; that flowers had bloomed in countless gardens, or that children had once played knuckle-bones, or some such game, perhaps in the very spot that he now stood. The water had either been transported by aqueduct, or there might have been fountains and wells. Higgotty was determined to find out which. He looked down at the object which had tripped him. It was a squarish piece of stone. The policeman scraped at the sand which half covered it and found a metal ring. A flush of excitement ran through Higgotty, following his discovering. Here, at last, was some hope! He took a firm grip upon the ring, using his handkerchief to protect his hands when he tugged. He pulled hard, but the stone was either too heavy for him, or was wedged fast, due to the amount of time it had rested there. Higgotty rubbed his chin, wondering how he was going to move the stone, or whether it was worth moving at all. Even though he felt hot and tired, he somehow knew that this was his last chance to find a way out of his predicament. Carefully he looked around. The ruins quivered in the heat haze as if they were alive; a broken statue appeared to beckon with its shivering arm. Higgotty closed his eyes.

'If this goes on much longer,' he muttered to himself, between clenched teeth. 'I shall go mad!' He opened his eyes; the heat and glare stung him. He wished he had brought his sunglasses; they would have provided some relief. Then he started, as if in surprise. To his left was a low crumbling wall. Higgotty moved over to take a closer look and found the remains of a camp fire; obviously travellers had used this spot to rest. They had even left a few miscellaneous items lying around. Then Higgotty jumped back in alarm. A grey shape had almost crawled to his feet. The word "snake" flashed through the policeman's mind. He backed away hastily, but the shape did not move, it continued to lie, sunning itself in the burning sunshine. Higgotty waited breathlessly, nervous that the beast had set a trap for him. The sun continued to burn through his shirt as he waited, and waited; but still the reptile did not move. Cautiously, the policeman inched forward. The greyish brown shape remained where it was, coiled upon the sand, motionless, as if it were dead. Without taking his eyes off the beast for even one second, Higgotty bent down and picked up a stone. Still the creature did not move. Taking careful aim, he threw his missile at the shape upon the sand. There was a dull "clonk" as the stone found its mark, but the snake did not move. Higgotty threw another stone, but without result. He grunted with satisfaction; the beast must be dead, he decided. He found a long stick by the remains of the camp fire. The policeman prodded the reptile cautiously, but it did not respond. Then Higgotty realised the truth of the matter. He gave a cry of astonishment at his own foolishness. The beast did not exist; it had been his imagination which had played tricks on him. He laughed, harshly, without mirth when his discovered his mistake. Perhaps it was the result of being turned into a snake himself which made Mr Higgotty more cautious of reptiles than most people would have been in similar circumstances. Throwing his stick away he gingerly picked up the "snake". He had found a piece of rope. Higgotty half-suspected Zardaka of placing the rope there to fool him. Coiling the length of rope around his arm, and carrying the largest and strongest piece of wood he could find, the policeman made his way back to the stone slab. First, he uncoiled his length of rope and attached one end to the ring. Then he took his piece of wood and tried to lever the stone up. There was an opening, just below the surface of the sand, where he could ease the tip of his stick. He heaved on the stick and felt the stone move slightly, but it was not enough, so Higgotty began to haul on his rope. With every muscle cracking in his body, the policeman felt the stone moving. He applied the wooden lever once more, before hauling on his rope. There was a grating sound, followed by a loud crash, causing Higgotty fall flat on his back. For a moment, he thought the rope had broken, but it hadn't. The stone had moved! There was a yawning hole, leading somewhere into the depths of the earth. He looked at the secret entrance with curious eyes.

'Well! Well!' exclaimed Higgotty, to no one in particular.

'Fancy that! Maybe I will find water after all.'

When he had recovered his breath sufficiently, he gazed down into the hole. Stone steps led downwards, and a musty kind of smell filled his nostrils. Higgotty wrinkled up his nose in disgust, but he knew he had no choice; either he went down those steps, or he could remain in the desert to fry to death. As if to remind him of his threatened fate, if he hesitated too long, the vultures still circled, watching him intently, hoping their expected meal would soon be ready. Higgotty shrugged. He coiled the rope about his waist, picked up his stout length of stick and slowly began to step downwards into the bowels of the earth. Although his progress was slightly ponderous, due to his weight, Higgotty's mind was fully made up and his did not hesitate for one moment as his heavy boots clumped their way down the stone steps, gritty particles of sand crunching underneath. He counted over two hundred steps before he reached the bottom. It was very dark down there, but comparatively cool after the brilliance of the Arabian sun. With outstretched fingers, Higgotty felt his way forward, his fingers scrabbling against rough walls and flaking plaster. The musty smell had increased, making him choke. Then to his horror, he felt something scuttle over his foot. Higgotty startled back in alarm; he had a fear of all creepy-crawly creatures and wondered if it could have been a scorpion. Desperately he pulled a box of matches from one of his pockets. Striking a match against the wall, the sudden light almost blinded him. Higgotty felt a scrabble of tiny feet moving away from him, and saw the pin-prick eyes, reflecting light from his burning match. His worst fears were confirmed; they were scorpions, but fortunately they appeared to be more frightened of him than he was of them. Then his match went out. Hastily the policeman lit another. He also pulled a page from his notebook and made it into a spill. Before the second match had expired, he had lighted his spill. To his great relief, the scorpions made no attempt to reach him. Higgotty began to tear pages from his notebook feverishly, and to make them into spills. He wondered what the Superintendent would have to say about his misuse of an official notebook for such a purpose! At first, Higgotty wondered if the steps only led as far as the chamber he found himself in, because wherever he shone his light, he only encountered a blank wall. There was no opening of any kind, but then his searching fingers encountered a projection. Striking another match, the policeman peered curiously at what he had found. The projection was in fact a metal object, which had been fastened to the wall. It was in the shape of a camel and looked as if it were made of gold. Higgotty's fingers explored the surface of the object and without thinking about what he was doing, he accidentally pressed down hard on the camel's hump. Instantly there was a creaking sound, and then the wall facing him swung away from him, as if it were hinged in some way. Higgotty didn't hesitate, he stepped into the opening, and no sooner than he had done so, the wall swung back into place and fastened itself with a sharp click. The policeman wasn't too happy over this. Desperately Higgotty felt the wall, trying to discover if he could re-open it, but he could not. As he made his way forwards something glinted on a ledge. To his delight he had found a primitive sort of lamp. It was a type he had never encountered before. He shook it gently; something splashed inside. Higgotty guessed that someone in the past had had the sense to fill the lamp with oil. Hastily, as his remaining matches were becoming alarmingly scarce, Higgotty lighted the lamp and a comforting glow filled the chamber. Higgotty felt relieved. So far, luck had been in his favour. He looked around curiously. The place he found himself in was a storeroom, filled with all sorts of items, such as kitchen utensils, ornate tables and chairs, armour, weapons and pots of all shapes and sizes, filled with precious stones.

Higgotty wasn't much of a historian, but he knew enough to realise that he was in the tomb of a dead person, who when alive had been of great importance. This discovery didn't exactly please Higgotty; there was something ghoulish about finding himself in a tomb, even if the dead person had been buried several thousand years ago, when the city above his head had been an important centre in a civilization, which had ruled most of the Ancient World. The storeroom's obvious purpose had been to supply all those things, which had been in use during the lifetime of the deceased, so that a comfortable existence could continue in the afterlife. The dead person would be lying in state in another room in the tomb, but where, and how one got there, Higgotty had no idea. He knew he would feel much happier when he could find food and water. With this thought in mind, he made his way to the end of the room and began to examine the walls and floor, looking for some key as to how this room fitted in with the rest of the tomb, or if there was some way out. Holding the lamp high above his head, his eyes caught sight of a metal ring in the floor, rather like the one he had found in the desert.

Higgotty didn't waste much time, every moment was precious to him. Unhooking his rope, he looped it through the metal ring and pulled with all his strength. The stone, much to his relief, began to move, slowly at first and then with increasing velocity. Soon there was another gaping hole, with another flight of steps for the policeman to descend. Winding the rope carefully back round his waist, the policeman cautiously began to descend. He this journey easier than the previous one, because he now had the lamp to guide him.

Much later he found himself at the bottom of the steps, picking his way over loose stones. Anxiously, Higgotty kept an eye open for scorpions, but to his relief there were none. Then he heard the trickle of water. Licking his dry cracked lips eagerly, he began to move towards the sound. His flickering lamp held high, he caught the reflection of black water, flowing swiftly through a tunnel, which looked as if it had been hewn out of the solid rock when the city had been young. As fast as he could hobble in his tight boots, Higgotty rushed forward. There was a stone platform, resembling a harbour quay, with steps leading down to the water. Obviously, in ancient times, this had been a secret port of some kind, probably connected with the tomb. Higgotty put down his lamp as carefully as he could, and then stumbled down the steps. He dipped his handkerchief into the water, and then squeezed it, so that the water fell into his open mouth, and splashed his hot face. He lay down on the steps and drank greedily, but he was careful not to drink too much. That would have been as bad for him as going without water in the desert all those hours. Drinking deeply for the last time, he looked about, half-hoping to find some vessel for carrying the water, but there was nothing he could use, unless he was prepared to go back to the storeroom for one and so he stayed close to the cold water, savouring the luxury of the precious liquid on his blackened tongue. Higgotty found his eyes begin to close with fatigue. He lay down and rolled himself into a comfortable heap on the quayside. Soon he was fast asleep.

Much later, something caused Higgotty to stir. For one awful moment he imagined he was back in the fountain, struggling against the water, drowning as the swirling torrent overwhelmed him, following the terrible blow that Mista the Owl had dealt him. Shapes appeared mistily before his eyes. He turned over, blocking out from sight these shadows which had appeared momentarily in his mind. It was just a bad dream, he told himself. Then Higgotty gasped as something hard jabbed itself against his ribs. He moved restlessly, half-awake and half-asleep, his body uncertain as to what was happening to it. The point of a spear pricked the sleeping policeman again. Higgotty moaned, realising for the first time that he wasn't dreaming. He opened his eyes fully, and suddenly wished he hadn't. His mouth fell wide open, as if to scream, but no sound came from his gaping mouth, fear paralysed him. In front of him torches spilt their flickering light on the stern faces of a score or more armed men. However, these soldiers were unlike any soldiers Higgotty had ever seen before. For one thing, they all wore armour and carried spears; short bladed swords hung at each man's side. The armour was not jointed and left the legs and arms partially unprotected. The lights the men carried gleamed coldly on their strange helmets and bronzed faces. Higgotty couldn't help the groan of despair which escaped his lips. He appeared to be acquiring a knack for getting himself into dangerous spots recently. A man, who was obviously in charge, snapped his fingers and two soldiers stepped forward, dragging the policeman to his feet.

'Hold on!' protested Higgotty. 'You've got no right to treat me like this. Let me go!'

The leader took no notice of his protestations. He said something in his own language, and pointed towards the river. For one awful moment, Higgotty wondered if the soldiers were about to throw him into the water. He shuddered and felt his legs go weak with fright. Then relief flood over him as he saw three soldiers spring to attention, salute their purple cloaked leader, and then rush off to carry out his order. Then the leader came over to Higgotty. The policeman was surprised to see the man was clean shaven, despite his strange dress. The leader grinned at Higgotty, showing his very white teeth.

'Marcus,' he said, stabbing himself in the chest.

Higgotty presumed this was the man's name.

'Marcus!' the man repeated.

'Marcus,' said Higgotty obligingly.

The leader was delighted with the policeman's response. He laughed and jabbed his finger at Higgotty and spoke a rapid sentence. Higgotty guessed Marcus wanted to know what his name was, so he told him.

'Higgotty?' Marcus repeated with great difficulty. Once again he snapped his fingers and grinning one of the soldiers approached Higgotty. He took something from a leather bag and made a little speech, then held out a small package. Cautiously Higgotty accepted what was being offered. To his surprise the package contained a few cakes. He tasted one with the tip of his finger; the cake was flavoured with honey. Impatiently the soldier indicated that the cakes were for Higgotty to eat. After he had finished, the soldier poured something for him to drink into a metal cup from a flask which hung around his waist. After that, Higgotty was taken down the steps at the quayside. At the bottom of the steps was a ship. It was elaborately decorated; an eagle made from beaten gold, acted as a figure-head, and there were other signs of the eagle at various points all over the vessel. The ship may have been small to twentieth century eyes, but there in the bowels of the earth, she looked huge. Slaves, with gold arm bands around their touch arms, waited with upraised oars, under the sharp eye of their slave master and his coiled whip. There was a canopy at one end of the vessel, and it was indicated by one of the men that this was where Higgotty was to sit. Then as soon as everyone was on board, the mooring ropes were untied. Because of the strong currents the ship shot away from the quay at a tremendous rate, making it relatively easy for the slave rowers to keep the vessel on course.

It was dark, except for the flickering torches which the soldiers carried. No talking was permitted, and all Higgotty heard from time to time was the voice of the ship master, giving his orders. Then there was the sound of water splashing against the wooden planks and the groan of the slaves, who were being taxed to the limits of their strength, as they were forced to pull against the contrary currents of the underground river. Eventually, Higgotty lost all track of time, as the ship ploughed on, hour after hour, relentlessly, without pause, wooden planks creaking, the chains of the slaves ratting against the dull thump of the oars. Higgotty could also hear the clink of the armed men as they shifted on their hard seats, trying to find a more comfortable position. Some of them were trying to snatch of few minutes' sleep; they had given their torches to companions and were taking it in turn to stay awake. Higgotty and Marcus were more fortunate; they had soft cushions on which to rest, and the canopy above their heads protected them from the icy blasts of air. With nothing to do, except watch the eerily lit faces, or the dancing flames playing upon the waves as they sped past the ship, Higgotty felt his eye-lids grow heavy and he fell asleep.

The next morning he was given some water in a small metal bowl, so he could wash himself. A piece of rough cloth was also supplied, so that he could dry himself. Another slave came with a sharp knife and shaved the bristles off Higgotty's chin. The slave also supplied Higgotty with a highly polished hammered sheet of metal, which could be used as a mirror. Marcus came over and told the slave to bring Higgotty a change of clothing. He was given a tunic, a red military cloak and a leather kilt. Before his own clothes were removed, Higgotty managed to transfer his precious notebook, matches and police whistle to the leather pouch he was given to wear. This was to be used in place of pockets. His truncheon, handcuffs and the length of rope, which he had picked up in the desert, were confiscated by Marcus, who viewed them as dangerous weapons. The rest of Higgotty's things were thrown overboard on the advice of the shipmaster, who was determined to carry only those things which had value. To pass time, the soldiers were engaged in sword practice, which wasn't anything like any sword fighting Higgotty had read about. Each man advanced on his adversary with a series of thrusts, which had to be parried. A trained swordsman did not cut or slash at his opponent, the swords were too short for that kind of work. Most of the practice sessions were carried out with wooden swords, so that no serious injuries took place.

Marcus and Julius spent much the time deep in talk, discussing something written on a parchment scroll, or taking elaborate readings of the sun with a variety of strange instruments, which Higgotty didn't even pretend to understand. The end of their voyage came suddenly one bright afternoon without any warning. One of the men keeping look-out began to shout. Marcus asked the man a question, and the man pointed towards the horizon, whilst

Paulinus, the ship master, and Julius consulted their chart. Higgotty stared towards the horizon. At first he could make out nothing, but as the morning wore on, he saw a bluish-grey smudge. He wondered what it could mean. Paulinus was jabbering away, excitedly pointing at the chart, the centurion nodding and hanging on to every word being said. Marcus began to issue orders, and Higgotty felt a general excitement begin to grip the ship.

The brisk breeze kept them on course all afternoon, until the evening, when it died away, but by that time they were within sight of what appeared to be a tropical island. Higgotty could smell spice in the offshore breeze. He heard a multitude of squawking birds amongst the foliage, where green creepers trailed about the luxurious flowers, so brilliant with colour, they almost glowed as they spilled their heavy scent across the water. Marcus, with uncharacteristic boisterousness, slapped Higgotty on the back and shouted something in his ear, which, of course, Higgotty didn't understand, but took it to mean that by morning they would all be going ashore. Behind him the soldiers were also gesticulating and laughing. Even the slaves look somewhat happier, because they would be allowed to go ashore, under guard, to stretch their legs and breath in some fresh air. In the morning, Higgotty was given a hurried breakfast, and then led across the deck to where the soldiers were preparing to disembark.

The ship was anchored as close to the shore as Paulinus dared go. It looked as if Higgotty was expected get his feet wet before getting ashore. The water reached up to Higgotty's arm pits. However, the sea was warm and quite pleasant to splash around in. Grinning, two soldiers grasped hold of the policeman and helped him towards the shore. In front of them the standard bearer walked, carrying the golden eagle of the legion on a long pole. Marcus and Julius came after him, each carried by four men in a pair of litters, which showed proper respect for their rank. After them trailed the other soldiers, making their way through the water as best as they could, cursing and coughing whenever a wave went up their noses or into their mouths.

Marcus then called the soldiers to order, and they began to march along the beach in tight formation, with Higgotty in the centre. One curious feature that the policeman noticed was that the soldiers did not march in step, but kept up a regulation pace by chanting a strange rhythm, urged on by their leaders.

Dawn and Stella

Dawn's father put down the paper knife he had been holding and fiddling with as he listened to Stella's incredible tale of how she had been abducted by Zardaka. Stella's voices began to falter as she reached the end of her story. 'The thing is' she said uncertainly, 'Well, I'm not sure as to what I should do next. If I go home, I shall get into dreadful trouble, because my parents won't believe me.'

Dawn exchanged a quick glance with her father.

'You see,' Stella stumbled on, 'Even Dawn found my story difficult to believe when she first heard it'

'I didn't!' Dawn snapped indignantly. 'It was just that I was so shocked to see you there I mean, you looked so strange and so alone. I didn't know what to think.'

'And so you think this rainbow has something to do with your escape?' asked Dawn's father, speaking for the first time.

He smiled kindly at Stella. If he had said something nasty or frowned at her, she would have burst into tears, but he didn't. Because of this, she guessed that somehow he believed her. A great wave of relief poured over her at this discovery.

'Yes,' she said softly. 'That rainbow bridges the gap between Zardaka's world and ours.'

'I'm certain it does,' said Mr Jennings sucking an empty pipe which he had picked up absent minded.

Stella stared at him incredulously.

'Oh yes!' Mr Jennings continued, seeing her startled look.

'I've heard of some very strange things which have happened in Back Lane over the past forty years.' He leaned forward and pointed at her with his pipe.

'We are going to find out just what Zardaka gets up to behind that garden wall of his.'

He began to stuff tobacco into his pipe furiously.

'Glass!' Dawn heard him mutter furiously. 'How dare they put such wicked stuff on top of that wall!'

'But what am I to tell my parents?' wailed Stella. 'They'll never believe me.'

'Truth is often stranger than fiction,' murmured Dawn.

'True enough,' agreed Mr Jennings. He searched his coat for matches.

'They'll say I'm making it up,' complained Stella. 'Only you and Dawn known that I'm not!'

'Hmn!' Mr Jennings began to light his pipe. 'This is certainly a problem, but I think I can solve it for you. Perhaps you ought to stay here the night, whilst I think out some solution which will suit both parties, then tomorrow we can break the news to the police and your parents that you have been found unharmed. How would that be?' His blue eyes searched her face. Stella's shoulders rose and then drooped as she sighed deeply. She stared helplessly at her friend.

'You choose what I should do,' she invited. 'I can think no longer.'

'Oh no, I can't,' Dawn said firmly. 'Only you can decide.'

Stella stared at the floor. 'Mother will be tearing her hair out with worry.'

'Then let me come with you,' suggested Mr Jennings. 'Maybe I can smooth things over; after all,' and his eyes danced mischievously. 'You wouldn't want a hairless Mother, would you now?'

'Oh, Father!' Dawn exclaimed in horror, half wanting to laugh.

'You do say the silliest things sometimes!'

Stella wasn't offended. To everyone's relief, she began to giggle. The thought of her mother becoming hairless over her disappearance was too funny for her to remain solemn.

'And you ought to come along as well,' said Mr Jennings to his daughter.

'Oh good!' Dawn shouted. 'I've got a spare coat which Stella can use, if she likes.'

'Thanks,' Stella said gratefully. She shivered. 'Brr! Don't you think it is unusually cold for this time of year?'

'It certainly is unusual for August,' Mr Jennings agreed.

Stella turned to Dawn. 'How many weeks are there before we go back to school?' she asked.

'Two,' Dawn answered promptly.

'Three months. I've been a prisoner of Zardaka for three months,' Stella said softly. 'You know, I really can't believe it.'

'Let's go!' said Mr Jennings putting on his coat. 'My! It is cold. If I didn't know it was August, I would say we were in for a spot of snow!' He laughed and knocked his pipe out, but Stella didn't laugh; she was horrified. Zardaka could, if he so decided, make it winter when it was summer, or spring when it should be autumn. Dawn and her father were so busy laughing that they didn't notice Stella's look of horror.

They called their farewells to Mrs Jennings and went outside. The trees were rustling in the avenue in which the Jennings family lived. It was a most mysterious sound, almost as if the trees were talking to each other. Stella felt a shiver run up her spine, which she didn't like it one little bit. It was almost as if the trees anticipated something strange happening. As she looked upwards, Stella noticed the sky was black, with only a little light coming from a pale moon. Strange dark clouds scudded upon their individual aimless journeys, sides glistening in the anaemic moon. Even the street lights, normally so powerful and effective, lacked their usual boisterousness. Stella and Dawn found themselves huddling together, half fearfully, progressing at a slouching crawl behind the large comforting bulk of Mr Jennings.

'Come on you girls! Whatever is the matter with you?' he grumbled. 'Oh, I know it's dark and cold, but it really isn't that bad.'

'That's what you think!' Stella muttered.

They had not gone far before it started to snow; heavy white feathers which fell thick and fast from the black and brooding sky. 'Snow!' exclaimed Mr Jennings, and he wiped a generous covering from his sleeve. 'I don't believe it! It is actually snowing in August!' He looked wildly all about him, up and down the street, but there was nothing living to be seen. All Mr Jennings could see were the heavy twirling flakes falling in an ever-increasing blinding shower. Soon the once wet glistening sheen of the street had disappeared under a thick noise-insulating carpet of blankness. Mr Jennings stood open mouthed. He tried to speak, but his words clogged up his throat, making him gasp and choke. He began to cough helplessly. Dawn thumped him on the back.

'What's wrong, Father?' she hissed.

'There's something funny going on here and I don't like it!' wheezed Mr Jennings. He coughed again and tears streamed down his face. 'What are we going to do now?'

Dawn glanced back down the road. There was nothing to be seen but the falling snow. 'Shall we go back?' she wondered.

'Why?' queried Mr Jennings. 'Why should we go back? We must be over halfway to Stella's house by now. No, let's go on. We mustn't waste more time.'

'I'm sure Zardaka is behind this,' Stella said.

'Why do you say that?' asked Dawn curiously.

'Because I think Zardaka has some reason, best known to himself, in stopping me getting back to my parents.'

Dawn felt a creepy sort of feeling crawl all over her body. Surely Zardaka didn't have this much power? Even as she wondered, the snow continued to fall, faster and faster, burying the pavements with white crystals. Before their very eyes the green leaves of the gardens grew heavy with white flakes and the grass could only show pathetic green spikes, which barely penetrated the soft mantle of wetness. Dawn moved her feet restlessly. There was the unfamiliar sound of crunching snow, then the coldness began to seep into her feet.

'Which way do we go?' she asked fearfully.

'This way,' said Mr Jennings.

'But we seem to have lost our way,' Stella argued. 'I don't think our house is over there. My house should be the last one on the right.'

As she heard Stella's words, Dawn felt another icy chill grip her heart and it wasn't the delayed effect of the snow! 'Are we lost?' she asked in a panic. 'Because if we are, please tell me?' She sounded so desperate for reassurance, that her father gripped her firmly by the hand. 'No, we aren't lost,' he said in the most confident voice he could muster. 'And we'd better get moving. You'll get cold standing here doing nothing.' He marched forward purposively, Stella and Dawn following reluctantly, not knowing where they were being led.

Stella felt especially uncomfortable, as the wetness beneath her feet began to slide into her silver slippers, making her lovely silk stockings wet, as the cold began to pinch her toes. She stamped her feet irritably.

After half-an-hour Mr Jennings had to confess that he was completely lost, even though, by his own estimation, they couldn't be more than three miles, at the most, from his own house. Somehow they had come out of the avenue into a road that no one remembered seeing before. The snow by this time was up to their ankles, and they were all feeling very wet, cold and slightly irritable. When they breathed, their breath snaked about their faces, like a white shroud, barely visible in the light which grew progressively dimmer as the street lamps continued to fade.

'Perhaps we could knock on someone's door,' suggested Dawn.

'At least we could find out where we are.'

'Maybe they would let us shelter until it stops snowing,' Stella thought.

'That's not a bad idea,' agreed Mr Jennings. 'At least it would put a stop to Zardaka, or whoever is responsible for this snow, playing games and generally messing us about.'

He snorted angrily. 'I've seen some daft things in my time,' he declared. 'But this beats the lot. Snow in August indeed!' He pointed wildly around him.

'As we are lost, let's knock on that door over there,' Dawn suggested practically. 'I don't know about the rest of you, but my feet are absolutely frozen.'

Mr Jennings and Stella looked at the door which Dawn had indicated. A modest privet hedge, white with snow, a garden gate and a narrow path across a neat lawn separated them from the green door. Funny pointed windows winked out at them in a most appealing fashion. If Stella had been more alert, she would have wondered where on earth she had seen such a house before, but her senses had been blunted by the cold and she couldn't be bothered to search her memory, even though alarm bells were ringing somewhere within her head.

'Come on!' urged Mr Jennings. 'Let's try it. I'm getting cold standing here.'

He opened the garden gate and marched up the garden path to the green door, his footprints dark and mournful, reflecting the blackness of the sky. Slightly worried about what might happen to them, the girls followed him. They were too cold and hungry with wandering about in the dark to linger outside the garden gate, even though all their senses told them that there was something terribly wrong

143

about the house. Dawn's father knocked hard upon the door. There was no answer, so he knocked again.

'Perhaps there is a bell somewhere,' suggested Dawn.

'Can't find one,' said her father shortly. He knocked for the third time, but there was still no answer.

'Now this is a puzzle!' exclaimed Mr Jennings. 'Lights on inside, but no one there to open the door.'

'Perhaps they're all watching television,' Stella wondered hopefully.

'Why don't we open the door ourselves,' Dawn said helpfully.

'That sounds a practical suggestion!' Mr Jennings agreed approvingly. 'Then if they demand to know why we have opened the door, we shall say: we thought you said to come in!' His eyes twinkled. 'There was so much noise from the television, you understand?'

The girls managed to smile for the first time since leaving the Jennings home.

'Do you think we really ought to open the door?' asked Stella. There was still a nagging doubt at the back of her mind, which she just couldn't place. 'After all, there have been some rather peculiar things happening lately,' she added. 'If you remember the boys went through a door and look what happened to them. And then I followed a kitten....' her voice trailed away. She ought to have been able to remember the rest, but she couldn't for some reason.

'I don't think you need worry about that,' said Mr Jennings soothingly, and he patted her on the shoulder. 'Nothing like that is going to happen this time. We are nowhere near Back Lane, if that is what you are thinking. Look! I'm going to knock once more and then I'm going to try and open the door. At least we can shelter until the snow has gone. Perhaps it is just some freak weather condition, which will soon pass.' So once again, Mr Jennings rapped on the green door. When there was no answer, he turned the handle gently. The door swung smoothly back on its hinges without a sound. 'Well! Just look at that!' invited Mr Jennings in amazement. The girls craned their heads to see what Dawn's father was seeing. In front of them was a small hall, with lights of various sorts, all shapes and colours, rather like Chinese lanterns, throwing out a garish pattern, which although unusual was in an odd sort of way comforting.

'Quite a little Aladdin's cave,' said Mr Jennings. His eyes were still wide with astonishment, but he was beginning to accept the unusual, in much the same way that Mr Higgotty, the policeman, had accepted everything which happened to him.

'Shall we go in?'

The girls nodded.

They entered the house. Soundlessly the door closed behind them. No one minded this much; at least they were out of the cold and wetness. As Dawn gazed about her, strange flickering lights seemed to pass over their heads, and mysterious whisperings sounded all around them.

'What the devil is going on?' demanded Mr Jennings.

'Something or someone touched my face!' squeaked Dawn.

'Do you know where we are?' Stella suddenly asked.

'Do you?' countered Mr Jennings.

'Zardaka's house.'

There was a stunned silence, whilst Mr Jennings and his daughter digested this information. Only the tinkle of the chandeliers and a humming sound from the strange lamps broke into the sudden hush. The flickering above their heads grew wilder and wilder, as the sinking and falling of the whispering grew in its intensity.

Mr Jennings was the first to break the uneasy silence.

'Let's get out of here,' he muttered. He ran towards the door, Dawn stumbling at his heels. Stella didn't bother to make the effort. She knew that flight was impossible, so she stayed exactly where she was. Dreamily she watched as Dawn and her father desperately tried to pull the door open. Just as she expected, it would not yield to their efforts and remained mysterious, if not obstinately shut.

'Aren't you going to help with this door?' Dawn shouted. Stella shook her head. 'What can I do?' she asked reasonably. 'You should know by now, it is far easier to enter Zardaka's world than it is to leave it.'

'But you got out.'

'By accident. That is how I met you.'

Dawn stared at her friend with a faint look of surprise. Stella was so unnaturally calm, it was unnerving.

'Just what are you up to?' Dawn asked suspiciously. 'Anyone would think you brought us here on purpose.'

'No. I didn't do that. But since we are here in Zardaka's world, it gives you both a good opportunity to see it for yourselves, and then you will know I was telling the truth.'

'I might have wanted the chance to see Zardaka's world,' Dawn replied, 'but I imagined I could just get into it and get out again, when I felt like it. I don't like the thought of being trapped in a place like this.'

'That's what worried me most,' said Mr Jennings. 'We don't know what he's like.'

'Welcome,' said a voice.

Mr Jennings jumped. The voice seemed to come out of nowhere.

Dawn grabbed her friend by the hand.

'What the dickens was that?' she cried.

'Ho! Ho! Ho!' the voice bellowed, echoing round the hallway, so that a porcelain pot actually danced upon its pedestal. The strange whispering became a deafening hum, causing the girls to put their hands over their ears, and Mr Jennings to screw up his eyes. A blue lightning streamer shot round the walls, making the air crackle with electricity.

'Ooh!' gasped Dawn holding on to Stella.

There was another spluttering crackle as a sudden streamer of vivid light illuminated the hall, making the windows rattle in their frames as the Chinese lanterns swayed back and forth, so that their light danced wildly into a kaleidoscope of bursting colours, which spread into an ever-growing arc, reaching out to span the four walls. Mr Jennings watched in amazement as the hallway grew to gigantic proportions; the ceiling rose to cathedral heights as the floor way spun beneath his feet, so that he momentarily lost his balance. When the swaying room settled at last, all three found themselves kneeling, facing a great multi-coloured band of light. The shimmering beads of light parted as a figure began to descend out of the rainbow. Mr Jennings gasped, because the man who stepped out of the rainbow was the tallest man he had ever seen. The man's long white beard stretched almost to his feet, and the cold expressionless eyes bored into their faces, making them shrink back, seeking fearfully to avoid the man's terrible gaze. The thin lips parted, the mouth opened and from the red cave, complete with curved teeth, came a booming laugh. Alighting from the rainbow, the man made his way slowly towards the kneeling figures. As he walked towards them, the man drew a tall pointed hat from his pocket, which he unfolded and then placed upon his head. A dark midnight-blue cloak billowed out behind him, like the wings of a great bat. Striding towards them, his feet hidden by clouds of smoke, the weird figure stopped before Mr Jennings.

'Who are you?' Mr Jennings sounded calm, but he didn't feel it. However, he felt he had to put on some show of bravery in front of the girls.

'Zardaka,' the figure said. 'Perhaps you have heard of me?' Mr Jennings nodded. Zardaka turned towards Dawn. 'And who is this?'

'My daughter.'

'Your daughter?' Zardaka's snake-like eyes glittered evilly.

'And Stella. Well…well! Here *is* a turn up for the book. The only person to find her way out of my world. Very clever of you, my dear, but I must make sure it doesn't occur again.'

'But what happened to Mr Higgotty?' Stella couldn't help asking, even though she knew Zardaka might not remember who he was, since turning him into a snake.

'Higgotty?' The wizard looked at her with a puzzled frown. 'Oh! You mean that frightful busybody, the policeman, of course!'

'Is he all right?' Stella inquired anxiously.

'All right?' The wizard rubbed his bony fingers together, making them crack alarmingly. 'All right? Hmn! I suppose it depends on what you mean by "all right"

148

doesn't it?' The wizard laughed an unpleasant kind of laugh, just as if he had invented some peculiar private joke.

'Suppose we stop playing games,' began Mr Jennings.

'You sir! You will only speak when you are spoken to!' rasped Zardaka.

Mr Jennings shrank back from the wizard's angry glare.

'As I was saying,' purred Zardaka, half to himself and half to Stella. 'It depends on what one means by "all right" doesn't it?'

'I suppose,' agreed the girl.

'Suppose you tell me what you know?' invited the wizard.

'Nothing much. Only that I fell into the fountain when Mista attacked us in the garden. When I woke up I found myself in a green meadow, with lovely summer flowers and birds singing.' Stella gave a deep sigh. 'I almost wish I was back there; it was so peaceful.'

She sounded so wistful, even Zardaka was moved to say: 'You may well return, at least someday.' Then his voice hardened into its normal harsh tones.

'Now, you must tell me everything you know. What do you think happened to Higgotty?'

Stella shook her head. 'I saw him fall into the fountain. I—I suppose he drowned. At least—well—I thought that for a while.'

'And what made you change your mind?'

'Well, despite everything that happened to me, I didn't drown and I can't swim—so I am not really sure what his fate was.'

149

'So he may still be alive?'

Stella nodded. 'I don't see why not.'

'Excellent! Excellent!' cackled the wizard, rubbing his long bony fingers together. 'So you were able to enter the wood from the sunny meadow?'

'Yes. That took me back to White Meadows.'

'Then you met your friend?'

Stella nodded, wondering where all this questioning was leading.

Zardaka stared blankly at the floor for a few moments.

'Come. I have something to show you.'

'What about my friends?' asked Stella in sudden alarm at the thought of leaving them. The wizard took her by the arm.

'Don't worry about them. They are perfectly safe here. I will see that no harm comes to them. You did say you wanted to find out what happened to Mr Higgotty, your policeman friend, didn't you?'

'Yes, and I also wanted to know what happened to Patch and the boys, Chris and Paul.'

Zardaka sighed. 'Ah yes! I was forgetting Patch. That was most unfortunate. You see, I don't really know what happened to him. The others are safe enough, but as for Patch…' He shrugged and left the remainder of the sentence unfinished.

Stella's heart sank at this, but she was somewhat relieved that at last she was going to find out what happened to Mr Higgotty and the boys. Zardaka led her along a long corridor, until they came to a winding staircase, which led to another corridor, and then to another set of stairs, not unlike the first. And so it went on, until poor Stella was dizzy and confused, which is perhaps what the wizard wanted to happen to her. Eventually, they reached a room. The room was bare, except for a large metal bowl, which stood on a pedestal in the centre of the room. Closing the door, Zardaka led the girl over to the bowl.

'Do not be afraid,' he said. 'No harm will come to you whilst I am here. Look into the depths of the bowl and tell me what you see.'

Curiously, Stella did as she was told. She gazed into the depths of the copper bowl. The green water was cloudy at first, and she could see nothing, but gradually it cleared. She heard a roaring sound in her ears, and glimpsed the blueness of the sea, which reflected light from a watery sun.

'What do you see?' asked the wizard.

Stella rubbed her eyes, making sure they were not deceiving her.

'I see—a ship!' she gasped.

'What else?'

'There are men on board and they're wearing some kind of armour and carrying swords. They have strange curved shields. They look like Romans to me.'

'Go on.'

'There is a man; he is making arrows. There are soldiers throwing something on the deck. I can't quite make out what. Now I see; they are playing dice.'

'What else do you see?'

'There are men rowing the ship, they have chains upon their legs. Oh! They are slaves. And there is a man with a whip. He looks very stern. he must be the slave master. The captain, he is seated in a chair talking to one of the men, who looks more important than the others.'

151

'Is there anything else?'

'A girl. She is with a man. She is dark and he is fair.'
Stella gasped.

'You know who the man is. Who is he?' demanded
Zardaka.

'It—it—it is Mr Higgotty!' Stella cried out in surprise.
'He is alive! I cannot see Patch with him. Only this girl.'

Zardaka smiled cruelly.

'Describe her.'

'She has long black hair; she wears gold jewellery
about her neck, rings upon her fingers, bangles on her arms
and legs. She wears some sort of tunic dress. Mr Higgotty
is wearing strange clothes too. They look home-made.'

'Do the soldiers wear the same clothes?'

'No. They are wearing leather kilts of some sort, tunics
with shiny breastplates over them. Some have spears, some
have plumes in their helmets, and all have short swords
and square shields, slightly curved. They are definitely
Romans.'

'How do you know that?' Zardaka asked curiously.

'Because I have seen them before, in a book.'

'So, they teach you such things at school?'

'Yes. Only, I forget most of it.'

'What do you see now?'

Stella resumed her gaze upon the water.

'There is a fog. I can see the golden eagle upon the sail
no longer. The slaves are rowing hard, but blindly. They
are lost; even the shipmaster does not know which way
they should go. Now there is a patch of light.' She paused
as if afraid to go on. 'I see—I see...Oh!' Stella fell back
with a groan.

'What is it?' the wizard demanded. His bony fingers gripped her arm fiercely. Stella tried to shake him off.

'Let me go!' she hissed fiercely.

'Tell me what you see—describe everything!' Zardaka demanded savagely.

'No! Look for yourself! Let me go!' Stella stormed. Tears began to well into her eyes.

'You will tell me everything!' Zardaka rasped. 'Or it will be the worst for you. Now!'

Tearfully Stella gulped once or twice and then looked back into the copper bowl. The ship was riding a gentle swell. The fog was only a memory now. A giant rainbow had looped itself around the vessel, which appeared to be oblivious to the danger it now faced.

'No! No! No!' Stella shrieked.

Even as she cried out in horror, she saw a giant whirlpool seize the ship in its mouth, dragging it into the centre of the rainbow. Stella saw the mouths of the soldiers and slaves open wide in terror as the planks of the ship burst asunder and the vessel was dragged beneath the waves. A green mountain of water, smooth and polished like glass, rose like a solid tooth, stretching itself towards the sky. Stella saw Higgotty and the girl stretch their arms towards her, desperately trying to call out to her, but no words or sound reached her, except the constant drone of the waves, which reminded her of the noise heard inside a shell. Then they were gone; the waves closed over their heads as the ship dropped like a stone beneath the waves.

'You!' sobbed Stella angrily. 'You—oh! You did that on purpose! You must have known what was going to happen, didn't you?'

Zardaka shook his head slowly. A faint smile played about his thin lips as he stroked his long white beard.

'No—I didn't know that would happen,' he said.

'You don't care—do you?' demanded the girl fiercely. She flung herself away from the copper bowl sobbing as if her heart would break. Zardaka waited until her sobbing subsided.

'Why do you cry?' he asked.

Stella didn't bother to answer.

'They are not dead,' the wizard said quietly.

Stella stopped crying.

'What?' she sniffed.

'I said: they are not dead.'

'Then why......?'

'There are many things you don't understand,' said the wizard.

Into the Jungle

The soldiers marched across the sand for a long time, and for the first time Higgotty was glad that he had retained his boots, and had not thrown them away, as he had been tempted to do so on more than one occasion. Then Marcus gave the order, and the soldiers responded by turning towards the jungle, which was to the left of them. Higgotty looked at the dense green wall which faced them, wondering how they were going to make their way through such a forest. To his surprise they did not have to cut their way through the vegetation, because a path already existed between the trees.

As they marched on, Higgotty felt the stickiness of the sweaty jungle closing in upon him, claustrophobic in its brooding intensity, as the sun, obscured by heavy leaves, resembled some bright jewel caught up in a cobweb, filled their faces with garish green light. Higgotty felt a shiver run up his spine, as he thought of the creepy crawlies living in the gloomy forest.

As if to lighten the gloom of the forest a little, flowers with garish clashing colours and heavy exotic perfumes, beckoned to the intruders with a luscious sweetness. The flower heads seemed to say: look at me! Am I not beautiful? But even these beautiful flowers had their spiteful side. Their big floppy leaves were wet with the recent morning downpour, and as the soldiers passed, anyone lax enough not to duck received a tepid shower, making them dance, curse or stumble. But there was no laughter from their companions, or jokes cracked at the unlucky person's misfortune; the forest subdued them all, with its brooding darkness and threatening intensity. The hum of tens of millions of insects was almost deafening, and Higgotty was forever being forced to stop and brush several tiny crawling creatures from his skin before they had a chance to eat him alive. Even the soldiers, who might have been expected to have become hardened against such conditions, were forced to slap the insects when their bites became intolerable. Somehow they struggled onwards. At mid-day they stopped for a short rest and meal. A couple of soldiers were sent to collect fruit and others to draw water from a nearby stream. Higgotty sat with his back firmly against the base of one of the friendlier looking trees. Now and then there was a wild chuckling high above his head, as some animal, maybe it was a monkey, scolded the busy soldiers. Higgotty felt his nerves begin to twitch, even the soldiers seemed alarmed; they all spoke in hushed voices and kept looking furtively around them. As for Marcus and Julius, Higgotty didn't like the way they kept looking at him and talking in whispers to each other. They were obviously discussing some plan, which involved the policeman. He wished he understood what they were talking about as he didn't like the sound of their talk one little bit.

By mid-afternoon the track they were following he disintegrated into marshland. Higgotty was given a spear, so that he could test the depth of the mud, before venturing too far into the slough. Gas bubbles arose wherever they put their feet, sending up putrid fumes, which made everyone hold their breath. Thick reeds grew everywhere, so that the soldiers and Higgotty were at times forced to make detours through the oozing mud. The policeman was worried that he might tread unwittingly on a snake, or something equally awful, but his fears were unwarranted. However, they did see three alligators sunning themselves by a deep pool. Marcus softly ordered them to make a wide detour, to avoid the brutes. By evening everyone was glad that the marsh was far behind them, and that they had started climbing a steep hill.

That night they made camp near some rocks. Huddled in his cloak, Higgotty felt the white marsh mist, which was drifting towards them, chill him. He was shivering so much that Marcus insisted that he should be given another dose of the raw spirit. Although Higgotty gagged as the evil liquid was forced down his throat, he had to admit that once it had been administered he felt much better. Cotta, one of the soldiers, who had given him cakes to eat and wine to drink, told him through a variety of signs that he was to sit closer to the fire. Higgotty was glad to do this, and the other soldiers made room for him round the fire. They were huddled in their army cloaks and were beginning to doze in the comforting warmth. Marcus had posted sentries, and each man was under orders to take a two-hour watch, whilst their companions snatched what sleep they could. Although they were only staying in the place for a short time, Julius had supervised the digging of rough fortifications, just in case an attack should come during the night.

When the sun came up the next morning, it looked as if it had dredged itself out of the marsh, which stretched out far below them. Higgotty was amazed to see the distance they had travelled through that awful place. Then he looked at the sun; it was pale and water-logged, cobwebbed with long streamers of white mist, which looked as if they had wrapped themselves around it. By the time the party were ready to move, the mist had mysteriously disappeared and the sun was once more its old self, having shaken off its early morning hangover.

An hour after breaking camp, it was warm enough for Higgotty to throw off his cloak. All about them, tiny jewels seemed to sparkle in the grass. This was the result of the heavy dew. Even as they looked, the jewels disappeared one by one into wisps of vapour as the sun gained its full strength. The soldiers were sweating in their armour, and Marcus was having to urge them on. It took them the best part of the day to reach the top of the mountain, and then the men were permitted to rest. Higgotty threw himself down panting; behind him he could see the ocean, stretching away into the distance, its deep blue merging with the horizon. Nearer the mountain, he could see the emerald flash of the jungle, and it seemed incredible that they had been able to walk all that distance only the day before. Marcus wouldn't let them rest long though. Higgotty had just enough time to catch his breath, drink a few mouthfuls of wine, eat a piece of very dry bread, before they were on their way again. By mid-afternoon they had reached a glassy plain. There was a strong wind gusting over the grass, making the stiff stems rattle and hiss like some ancient steam locomotive. Marcus forced his men to run across the plain, only allowing the briefest of pauses, so that Higgotty could catch his breath. After two hours of alternatively running and walking, Higgotty spotted smoke in the distance. He guessed that there were people living on the plain and that the smoke was from their cooking fires. Soon they came within sight of some round huts within a stockade made from thorn bushes. The stockade was to protect the village from wild animals. The huts were mean and poor, made from grass and mud, with stick walls. Some men came running out of the village to greet the soldiers. All of them were fair skinned and carried heavy spears, in contrast to the much lighter spears which Marcus's men carried. Every man wore a grass skirt and very little else, except for decorative bangles about their arms and necks. Higgotty wondered if Marcus on some previous visit, had supplied some of the jewels which made up the necklaces.

Marcus and Julius went forward to greet the men. One man, wearing several ostrich feathers, and much more precious jewellery than the others, appeared to be the chief, because the Tribune greeted him with great deference. The chief's name was Tarkus. He greeted Marcus and Julius with a handclasp, their hands gripping each other's forearms, in the Roman manner. At a signal from Marcus, two soldiers stepped forward. They carried a heavy chest, which they placed at the feet of the native chief. Marcus unlocked the chest himself, and threw back the lid. There was a murmur of excitement from the villagers who had crowded round to stare at the strangers. Even Tarkus was suitably impressed at the profusion of jewels and coins which met his gaze. He nodded and said something to Marcus, who smiled. Then the lid was closed and the chest locked. With great ceremony, the Tribune then presented Tarkus with the key to the chest. The key

159

was on a slender silver chain, so the chief could wear it round his neck for safe keeping.

Marcus then signalled to his men. They were to present Higgotty to the chief. Tarkus looked into the grim face of the policeman and asked him a question. Higgotty shrugged, trying to signify that he did not understand. The chief began to speak rapid sentences to Marcus. Higgotty heard his name mentioned more than once during the conversation between the chief and Tribune; it was obvious that Tarkus was being told how the policeman had been found. Then the centurion made Higgotty open his mouth, so that the chief could inspect his teeth. Tarkus then felt Higgotty's muscles and tapped his chest. Higgotty couldn't help smiling, wondering what Inspector Gleeson would say if he could see him now! Again the chief fired a question at him, but Higgotty shook his head in a stupid sort of way to show he didn't understand what was being said to him. Angrily the chief stamped his foot and shouted at Marcus. Tarkus seemed to be in a thoroughly bad mood about something. Eventually, the Tribune got Tarkus to calm down by offering the chief one of the spare lances which the soldiers carried. Sulkily the chief agreed to accept this. Then it was smiles all round, and the party could enter the village in triumph. Higgotty was taken away and put in a hut of his own. As he went Julius shouted something to him, which Higgotty presumed was some sort of farewell. Wearily he waved his hand, indicating that he understood what was happening; he had been presented as a gift to the native chief Tarkus.

As he was too tired to bother to work out what was happening to him, Higgotty lay down on the floor of the hut, which to his relief was clean and tidy, and went to sleep. Much later he felt someone touch his arm. Opening his eyes he saw a young girl sitting before him. She brought him some food to eat and a drink which tasted like beer. Higgotty gratefully accepted all that was set before him. When he had finished, the girl silently removed the empty vessels and Higgotty went back to sleep.

For several days Higgotty was kept in the seclusion of his hut. Occasionally, someone of importance in the village would come to visit him, but they did not attempt to speak to him. They only came to stare and remark on the whiteness of his skin to their friends. The girl came every day to feed him, but beyond her shy smile, Higgotty got no response to his questions, except that her name was Nadira. On the fifth day, following his arrival in the village, Higgotty was taken to a nearby forest and set to work with other slaves. He was ordered to gather fruit and it was hard work. Higgotty was given a wicker basket, which took half-an-hour to fill. When it was filled, he carried it over to the overseer, who watch whilst he emptied the contents into a larger container, to be dragged back to the village by Tarkus's slaves. There was no rest; as soon as his basket was empty, Higgotty was expected to go back for more. By the end of the day Higgotty's head was aching from the sun, and his back was sore from constant lifting, or scrabbling about on the floor in pursuit of fruit tossed down to him by fellow slaves. Sometimes, for a change, he was sent to gather nuts, but the basic routine remained the same. Every evening the prisoners were driven back to the village; the slaves to sleep in their communal hut, and Higgotty in his own personal quarters. This special treatment may have had something to do with the fact that the policeman was no ordinary slave, but a gift from the Tribune to Tarkus. Eventually, on returning to his hut in the evening, Higgotty became too tired to eat what the girl brought him. Apart from telling him that her name was Nadira, the girl had refused to speak to him, although, she looked concerned when he refused to eat.

Each succeeding morning became a nightmare of similarity for him. Every morning he was woken at dawn and led to the forest. There was always something for him to do; his captors saw to that. If he wasn't employed collecting fruit, Higgotty was busy on the plain, cutting long bunches of grass to be used for thatching the mean looking huts which housed the villagers. Higgotty knew that if something didn't happen soon, to end this terrible slavery, he would go mad. Then one night the girl came to his with his meal as usual. When she saw he wouldn't eat, she looked at him sorrowfully.

'What is wrong?' she asked. 'Why don't you eat. See, I have prepared the food with my own hands.'

Higgotty stared at Nadira in amazement. For a moment he was so surprised he could not speak.

'You speak English,' he said. 'How is that?'

Nadira smiled. 'I was taught to speak your language by my mother; she was a slave like you.'

'Aren't you a slave?'

Nadira shook her head. She had long glossy black hair, creamy brown skin and very dark eyes. Looking at her properly, for the first time, Higgotty realised that she wasn't of the same race as the other villagers. He wondered where she came from.

'My mother came from a part of South America, I think,' the girl explained. 'She was a slave, but I am not. Soon I shall be married to Tarkus.'

'The chief? But I thought he was already married.'

Nadira put her finger to her lip, and went to the entrance of the hut. She lifted the curtain, which served as a door, but there was no one about.

'You must be very careful not to offend Tarkus,' she warned the policeman.

'How do you mean?'

'Never speak to me if the guard is waiting outside your hut. Whenever I bring you your food, the guard goes off for his. When he does that, we are safe, but he will be back within the hour.'

'What is all this about you getting married?' demanded Higgotty.

'I shall be married within the month,' Nadira replied softly. 'But you are right; Tarkus is married; I would be his fourth wife and not as respected as the others.'

'Do you want to marry him?'

Nadira looked at Higgotty scornfully. 'What do you think?' she asked.

The policeman remained silent. 'I tell you, he is an evil man,' Nadira hissed. 'Within a year I shall be dead, just like all those other young girls he has picked up and then discarded. I do not want that.'

'I don't suppose you do,' Higgotty said uncomfortably. What the girl had told him sent a shiver down his back. All the time Nadira had been speaking, his mind had been a whirl. He was thinking desperately, trying to find a way out of his predicament.

The girl looked at him thoughtfully.

'Do you want to escape?' she asked.

'What was that?' Higgotty leaned forward in his excitement.

163

'I will help you escape, but you must trust me. Say nothing about what I have said to anyone else. Is that understood?'

Higgotty nodded.

'Yes—I understand,' he said.

'If you don't keep silent, then I might be killed!' the girl added fiercely.

'I understand,' Higgotty repeated.

'Good!' whispered Nadira. There was a noise outside. She started back in fear.

'Remember what you promised. Now I must go!' she hissed.

As she gathered up the empty pots, Nadira gave the policeman a reassuring look. 'Don't worry, I shall return.'

Higgotty didn't see Nadira again for two whole days. He wouldn't admit it, but he was worried for the girl's safety. For the first time since his arrival in the village, be began to feel sorry for someone other than himself. He wanted to help the girl, if he could, just as he had wanted Stella to escape Zardaka. During the time Nadira was away, a rather sullen looking girl brought Higgotty his meals. Although the policeman was friendly towards the new girl, she never really spoke properly to him, or gave him any encouragement, so he didn't know if he could trust her enough to ask a question about Nadira. He was in a fever of impatience to see Nadira again; on the third day she re-appeared. Higgotty had been dozing on a pile of sweet smelling straw when the Nadira entered the hut without any warning. Through half-open eyes he saw Nadira put his meal down on the floor for him. She made no move to leave, but remained squatting on her heels. Although Higgotty felt exhausted from working in the jungle, he managed to sit upright, after making several unsuccessful attempts.

'So you're back. Thought you had gone for good,' he said in an ungracious sort of voice, determined to show some streak of independence. Although all he really wanted to do was throw his arms about the girl, he was so pleased to see her again.

'Corn. I cooked it myself.'

Higgotty grunted.

'Eat it now,' the girl insisted. 'Whilst it is still hot.'

'Are you the only person in the village who speaks English?'

Nadira said nothing, so Higgotty picked up the wooden fork and began to eat. When he had finished, Nadira took away the clay pot and returned with a stone jug for him to drink from.

'What is that?' Higgotty asked suspiciously.

'Native beer. Our men like it—I thought you might.'

'I'd rather have a cup of tea.'

Nadira smiled for the first time.

'Are all the English the same?' she inquired. 'All cups of tea and cucumber sandwiches?'

Higgotty laughed.

'Aren't you going to ask me where I have been these last few days?' the girl asked reproachfully. Her red lips pouted. Higgotty thought it a very attractive pose.

'Sorry!' he apologised hastily. 'Of course I was.'

'Yes. Far more interested in what I had brought you to eat, than in seeing me again,' Nadira interrupted scornfully.

'Hold on!' Higgotty protested. 'That really isn't fair!'

'Tell me what is fair then?' Nadira challenged.

'I was going to ask the other girl about you.'

Nadira stiffened, as if with fright.

'Describe her!' she insisted sharply.

Higgotty described Nadira's substitute.

'I hope you didn't say anything to her.'

Higgotty sensed the panic in her voice.

'Of course I didn't,' he reassured her. 'I tried to make conversation, but she ignored me. Do you know her?'

'Do I know her?' the girl echoed bitterly. 'Yes, I know her!'

'Who is she then?'

'Tarkus's daughter.'

'Good heavens!' Higgotty felt quite shocked.

'She was spying on us,' Nadira said in a flat sort of voice.

'And I was thinking of asking her about you.'

Nadira looked horrified.

'Of course, I didn't ask her!' Higgotty almost shouted. 'I didn't know if I could trust her and then I remembered your warning about not speaking to anyone.'

Nadira suddenly relaxed.

'You weren't to know who she was,' she said kindly.

'How do you know she's not spying on us this very moment?' Higgotty asked curiously.

'Because Marcella, that's her name, has gone away with Tarkus on some business for a few days.'

The girl thought for a moment or so.

'You know, we are quite safe; we can make our plans whilst they are away.'

'What plans?' Higgotty wanted to know. 'And what happens if anyone should suspect us?'

Nadira shrugged. 'So what? The result will be the same; stay here and you will die. You escape, and if you allow them to catch you, you will die. Do you want to stay here and die of overwork, or do you want to take a chance? As for me, I will die anyway. Even thinking of escaping is a crime here.'

'Surely not!' Higgotty said in alarm.

'What does it matter?' Nadira asked. 'I may as well die now, in helping you to escape, as wait till I am married to that—pig!' Nadira spat out the last word with real venom. 'The result of being married to Tarkus is always the same. I told you that before. I may live for a few years, but eventually I shall die.'

'But you could escape with me!' Higgotty suggested.

'I shall have to,' Nadira agreed. 'The longer we both stay in the village, the more danger we will find ourselves in. Tarkus's wrath is legendary.'

'How do you mean?'

Nadira sighed. 'There are plots, always secrets, and then there are even more plots. You will find out, if you stay around, but you're not going to do that. You are going to escape because I have a plan.' Carefully she explained her plan to Higgotty.

'There is no time to lose,' the girl added, as she gathered up the empty pots.

'Tarkus will return after tomorrow, with his horrible daughter, Marcella.'

Nadira flashed a sudden look at Higgotty.

'I hope you haven't fallen in love with her,' she said softly.

'What!' Higgotty was genuinely shocked. 'As if I would!'

'That is good,' she said approvingly. 'Then we go tomorrow. It will be our first and only chance.'

'I shall die if I stay working in that plantation,' Higgotty admitted.

'You would die even most horribly, if you messed around with Marcella!' Nadira warned. 'Tarkus wouldn't like it one little bit. So don't say I didn't warn you!'

Higgotty opened his mouth, as if to protest.

'Oh, don't mind me and my petty jealousies!' said Nadira. 'What I mean is, you will die, once Tarkus gets tired of seeing you around the place.' She got to her feet and took the jug away from him.

'I must go. They will miss me if I stay any longer. I will be waiting for you in the forest tomorrow; I know where to go.'

Before Higgotty could do anything to stop the girl, Nadira had thrown her arms around his neck and kissed him briefly on the cheek. Then she had gone, slipping into the night like a shadow. For the first time since Marcus had left him alone to his fate, Higgotty felt his heart grow lighter. It was an easy mind that he fell asleep that night.

The next morning his day started in the normal way. The guards marched the slaves into the jungle, much to Higgotty's relief, because he knew that escape from the grassy plain would be much more difficult. After an hour of collecting fruit, Higgotty Nadira give the pre-arranged signal; she was whistling like one of the birds which inhabited the forest. Higgotty was accustomed to the high-pitched whistle of this particular bird, so he had no difficulty in distinguishing the signal. Looking all around him, making sure that he was no being observed, Higgotty chose carefully his moment to leave the rest of the slaves. He flung his basket into the bushes, taking care to throw it where it could not easily be found by the overseer. One of the slaves saw Higgotty take to his heels, but said nothing, only gazed after him with vacant eyes. Most slaves accepted their fate; the alternative was very horrible to contemplate.

Nadira saw Higgotty coming down the forest track. She lifted her head and whistled again. The policeman changed his direction and made towards her. Nadira was crouched against a tree. Higgotty only had to take one look at her to know that something was wrong.

'What is it?' he hissed. 'Tell me?'

He shook Nadira, because at first she would not answer, due to the fact she appeared to be in a state of shock. When at length she managed to speak, it was as if she were out of breath. Her news was, as the policeman had half-expected, was very bad. Marcella had sent out an order on behalf of her father that Nadira was to be arrested and tried for treason. Marcella was to act as both judge and jury. There was no doubt in Nadira's mind that Marcella would have had her executed, had she lingered in the village any longer. The actual details of the crime Nadira was alleged to have committed were not clear, nor did they matter, the result was always the same and death was the reward for treachery against Tarkus.

'Now do you still love her?' the girl finished.

Higgotty shook Nadira hard. 'Stop saying that!' he said full of anger. 'For the last time, I never spoke to that wretched Marcella. Do you hear? Never spoke to her!'

Nadira closed her eyes as if she wasn't sure whether she believed him or not.

'How can she suspect you, especially when she hasn't a shred of evidence against you?' protested Higgotty.

Nadira gave him a withering look.

'Marcella doesn't need evidence,' she reminded him scornfully.

'She just wants to get rid of me, therefore she will use any excuse. You were the best one she could think of.'

'Thanks very much!' Higgotty said sarcastically.

'Only, it was a lucky guess on her part, because it happens to be true.'

'The policeman thought about this for a moment, then pulled Nadira to her feet. 'Come on!' he ordered. 'I think it is high time we got out of here.'

As they hurried through the jungle, Nadira told Higgotty one or two more details of what she had learned in the village that morning.

'Murtaza, that is the man Tarkus left in charge of the village, he's a good friend of mine. He tipped me off and told me to get away, as far away as I could from the village. I am to wait in the jungle until he sends word.' She gave Higgotty a wry sort of smile. 'Only we shan't be there.'

'We?' the policeman queried with a puzzled look upon his face.

'With your help I shall be soon far away,' Nadira explained. 'Murtaza told me where I should go.'

'How do you mean?'

'The ship!' the girl said. 'That's where we are going.'

'The ship? You said nothing about it yesterday.'

'Didn't I?' Nadira asked with a shrug of her pretty shoulders.

170

'Marcus may have sailed away by now,' Higgotty objected.

'I don't think so,' Nadira said confidently.

Higgotty looked at her sharply. 'You know something?'

'Maybe I do, and then maybe I don't!' She said cheekily.

'Why you little scamp! Wait until I catch you!'

Nadira gave a giggle and flew down the path, Higgotty in hot pursuit.

She was lighter on her feet than the policeman and soon left him far behind. Eventually, they both were tired of running in the heat, but the chase had served its purpose; they had covered more distance than Higgotty would have thought possible in the circumstances. 'What do you mean about the ship?' Higgotty asked Nadira, when he had regained his breath. He mopped his face, the run through the jungle had made him extremely hot and tired.

'Can't you guess?' Nadira asked She looked as cool and collected as the first time Higgotty had met her.

'No, I can't guess!' Higgotty said crossly. 'I'm no mind reader.'

'That's a relief,' muttered Nadira. 'Well, I thought it might be an idea for us to get on board and sail with them.'

Higgotty's eyebrows rose in astonishment. 'You must be mad!' he exploded. 'Marcus would hand us straight back to Tarkus.'

'Would he? I'm not so sure he would.'

'How can you know that?'

'I know,' she replied simply. 'Think about it.'

Higgotty did think about this for some time, before venturing to speak. 'You might have something there,' he said. 'I was a gift, but I don't think slavery was quite the way Marcus intended me to be used.'

'Keep thinking on those lines,' Nadira said briskly. 'There is no "might" about my plan; we'll get away from this place, if you can find your way back to the ship. In any case, the Romans do not approve of wives being executed by their husbands.'

'Show me where the mountain is,' Higgotty demanded, 'and then I can guide the way back to the ship. Are we far from the mountain?'

'No. You don't have to worry about that. Just follow me.'

There were no sounds of pursuit yet, and Higgotty began to feel more confident.

'You know,' he said after they had walked a long way in silence, 'if Marcus was to hand us back to Tarkus, it would make him look like an accomplice. By that, I mean, Tarkus would suspect Marcus of setting the whole thing up.'

Nadira nodded. 'Of course he would: Tarkus thinks suspiciously of everybody. Even Marcella, his own daughter, and if he were Marcus…'

'He would expect Marcus to plot and scheme in the same way.'

'Exactly!'

'Of course,' Nadira mused. 'Marcus wouldn't do exactly as Tarkus would do.'

'Wouldn't he?'

'That's because Marcus wouldn't want to spoil his chances of coming back to this island again.'

'Just what is Marcus after?' Higgotty asked curiously.

Nadira shot the policeman a surprised glance.

'Pearls, sandal-wood, or anything his people consider valuable.'

'Slaves?'

'Sometimes.'

'Sounds like a perfect gentleman,' sneered Higgotty.

'But he gives Tarkus a great deal in return.'

'Are you sure?'

'Well,' Nadira said uncertainly. 'They were almost at each other's throats the last time they met, because of some dirty trick which Tarkus played on Marcus. You were a sort of peace offering. Marcus knows that Tarkus likes to have an educated man, like yourself, working for him.'

'You could have fooled me!' Higgotty snorted.

'But when he found out you could not speak his language… that is why Tarkus was disappointed in you. Besides, that, most of the people of this island would like to trade freely with Marcus, but they are not sure if he can be trusted.'

'So what are you saying, Marcus is as bad as Tarkus?'

'Worse. Marcus called himself "civilised" and so he should know better, but in his eyes Tarkus is the simple savage. Oh yes! I know Tarkus cheats Marcus, but Marcus cheats Tarkus.'

'Then I was right. They are as bad as each other.'

Nadira thought over the policeman's remark.

'The only difference I can see is, I don't think Marcus would steal back something he had given Tarkus, especially, if it were a peace offering. That would be begging for trouble. I don't think Marcus wants that.'

'How is it you know so much about Marcus?' Higgotty asked curiously.

'I was an interpreter for Tarkus once. I had been on board Marcus's ship and was responsible for taking him to some of the nearby islands. Those islands which pay tribute to Tarkus. You see, I was there to smooth negotiations for Marcus, do you understand? Anyway, I taught Marcus our language.'

'But he doesn't speak English,' Higgotty objected.

Nadira frowned. 'How could he? You and I are products of another age. English doesn't exist in his time scale, but for some reason I am able to communicate with him.'

'Just how much do you know about time?' Higgotty asked.

'A great deal and although I have not heard your full story, I can read in your eyes and face that you are from a different time, just as I am. But there must be a difference, because I can communicate in Latin and you can't.'

The policeman looked sceptical. He knew Latin was a dead language, but there were professors and intellectuals who could communicate in it. Nadira continued.

'I told you my mother came to the island, but I didn't tell you she was from a different age. No, I don't know how she got here, but I do know that some very strange things have happened here. I did not understand them all at first, but seeing you and Marcus, and the others makes me think I shall discover the truth eventually. Perhaps you would like to tell me your story?'

Higgotty promised he would, but only when it was time for rest. They must move on as fast as possible to put as much distance between themselves the village.

By evening, they had reached the lower slopes of the mountain. They had taken a different route from the one

174

followed by Marcus. Nadira guessed that Marcella would be expecting them to try and escape across the grassy plain, because it was the easier route. She would not expect them to try the more difficult route through the jungle. There was no doubt in Nadira's mind that Marcella would have placed her warriors near the grassy plain, in the hope of catching Higgotty and herself. Nadira couldn't help smiling when she thought of the way she had outwitted her hated rival; also how much it would hurt Tarkus's pride when he found that Higgotty had not been apprehended. 'What are you smiling about?' Higgotty asked in a grumbling sort of voice. 'I don't see anything to laugh about.'

'Of course you don't, you poor old dear!' Nadira gripped his arm with a friendly sort of squeeze. 'I expect you are missing the cucumber sandwiches,' she whispered wickedly. 'Never mind; soon you will be home in time to have a cup of tea with the vicar.' Higgotty laughed out aloud at this, and pretended to clout Nadira on the ear.

'I bet you don't know what a vicar is, less what he does.'

Nadira hugged him in delight.

'You know very well I don't!' she admitted. 'Much of what my mother told me made no sense. In fact, it was only words. Sometimes, I think I dreamt half the things she told me.'

Higgotty looked at the sun.

'I hate to rush you, but shouldn't we be making camp soon? It will be dark soon.'

'By the way,' Nadira said, after she and Higgotty had made camp, 'What was the name of Marcus's ship?'
'It's called the *Jupiter*, I think.'

'Then we have no time to lose!'

'What on earth do you mean?'

Nadira gripped the policeman by the arm.

'Listen to me! I heard a man in the market place, only this morning, say that Tarkus was determined to destroy *Jupiter*. Because I had my own worried to think about, I didn't take too much notice at the time. Do you understand?'

'Are you saying we ought to warn Marcus?'

'Yes. He and Julius may be so grateful, they will welcome us on board.'

'I think you might have told me all this a bit earlier,' Higgotty grumbled.

'I told you! I had problems of my own. Not least my rescuing you. Or had you forgotten?'

'I'm sorry,' Higgotty apologised. 'Do go on.'

'Well, as I say, we can prove ourselves good friends to Marcus. What do you think?'

'Has Tarkus ever made threats against Romans before?'

'Not as far as I know. Someone said that Tarkus would burn them all.'

'Everyone?'

Nadira nodded. 'All the slaves and everyone aboard *Jupiter*.'

'It sounds foolish talk to me,' Higgotty said sceptically.

'I don't think so. You don't know what Tarkus is capable of.'

'Are you sure this will happen, or is it just village gossip?'

'I overheard everything,' the girl said sullenly. 'You don't have to believe me if you don't want to.'

'I didn't say that; but how do you know it wasn't just idle talk?'

'I've already told you. It is just the sort of cowardly thing that Tarkus would do,' Nadira hissed defiantly.

'All right! All right! Keep your hair on,' Higgotty soothed.

Nadira felt her hair curiously; it was as if she expected it to be loose on top of her head. 'What was that you said about my hair?' she inquired.

'Oh that! It was just a figure of speech,' Higgotty tried to explain.

Nadira looked at him with a bewildered sort of look.

'A figure of speech? What's that?'

'I mean,' Higgotty floundered. 'It means: don't get in a temper.'

'I'm not!' grumbled the girl crossly. 'You won't believe me when I tell you Tarkus is jealous of Marcus.'

'Why?'

'Tarkus has always been jealous of the "metal men". He calls them that because of the armour they wear. Do you understand?'

Higgotty said he did. Nadira continued.

'You know, the Romans make such pretty things. The men in the village, they are jealous, and yet they cannot match the skill of Marcus's craftsmen.' She sighed. 'How I wish I could get someone to make me pretty jewellery like that!'

'Tell me more about Tarkus's plans.'

Nadira frowned. It was as if she resented the interruption.

'Oh that,' she said, as if it had no bearing on what was happening.

'Tarkus has this scheme, and it's such a crazy idea, he wants to defeat the Romans and take over their culture. He doesn't understand, or even want to know, that there are many thousands of these Romans living many miles away, who would take revenge on Tarkus if he committed such a foolish act.'

'What act?'

'Oh, stealing everything,' Nadira said vaguely. 'Don't you want something to eat,' she said, changing the subject.

Higgotty said he didn't.

'Why don't you go on with your story?' he invited.

'I haven't anything more to say,' Nadira said sullenly. 'In any case, you promised to tell your story. I have a feeling your story holds some sort of clue, something which could help explain everything which has happened on this island.'

Higgotty, rather hesitantly at first, but more fluently as he became engrossed in his tale, told Nadira everything he knew, from the time he had sighted Chris and Paul in Back Lane, accused of robbing a supermarket, to the moment he had entered Zardaka's garden. Eventually, a great weariness overtook them both, and they both lay down by the fire and fell fast asleep.

Daybreak saw them hurrying as fast as they dared, across the boulder strewn landscape, zigzagging up the trees, slipping and sliding, breaking fingernails, sometimes narrowly missing breaking some bones, as they raced their way to the top of the mountain. They were trying to put as much distance between themselves and Tarkus as possible. Even when they had scaled the peak, neither of them dared pause for rest or food, such was their hurry to reach the comparative safety of the marsh. Very few of Tarkus's men would venture there; it was rumoured to be an enchanted place. To more practical thinking people, there were very real horrors lurking there, more frightening than the rumours of magic, mythical beasts or unspeakable demons. Nadira wasn't particularly frightened by the marsh, but she was not exactly happy about being up to her knees in mud.

As Higgotty didn't relish the thought of staying overnight in the forest, so they kept going. The policeman, more by fluke than good judgement, stumbled across the path, and this had influenced his decision to keep going. Even then, their troubles had not ended. They found themselves stumbling along the path, bumping into trees in the gloom, the moon not helping much, because of the density of the trees growing overhead. Exhausted, trembling with weariness, parched with thirst, they somehow managed to make the beach by dawn, and lay down on the sand to rest.

Attacked!

Their rest was to be short-lived, however, some mysterious crabs came sliding over the beach towards them, sensing a meal of some sort. Higgotty and Nadira, not wishing to become breakfast for the crabs, were forced on, until they were within sight of Marcus's ship *Jupiter*. The man on board *Jupiter* rubbed his eyes in disbelief; two ragged scarecrows were picking their way carefully along the beach. He gasped sharply, gripping the wooden rail tightly. Surely one of the people was familiar? He squinted in his effort to make out more details. Yes, it was the man they had found under the city of Tiveria, but who was the other person? Was it a woman? He called softly to his companion, who tip-toed softly away to notify Julius that they had visitors. Wearily Nadira and Higgotty waded through the water. The ship appeared to be deserted. Higgotty wondered if something had happened to the crew; perhaps Marcus and Tarkus had already double-crossed each other? Then again, maybe the whole crew had been murdered? Higgotty shuddered at the thought. He grasped a trailing rope and began to haul himself aboard. No one tried to stop him as he stepped on to the wooden deck. Nadira was still struggling up the rope, so he turned to help her. As he straightened up again, having hauled Nadira safely on board, his stomach contracted with fear;

the sharp point of a spear was pointing directly at his midriff. He heard Nadira gasp as strong arms grasped her.

'Bring them over here,' commanded a familiar voice. It was Marcus. Of course, Higgotty didn't understand what was being said, but Nadira did, and later she could translate the conversation which took place between her and Marcus.

The grim-faced soldiers marched Higgotty across the deck to where Marcus sat. Julius, looking suitably bored with the whole affair, set next to the Tribune, fanning himself with a large palm leaf.

'Well! Well!' Marcus marvelled. 'Cast your bread upon the water and it will return.' At least, this is the way Nadira translated what had been said.

'Your gift to Tarkus has returned two-fold,' Julius observed sourly.

Marcus beckoned Nadira forward.

'Don't I know you?'

'Of course you do,' she retorted.

Julius frowned. Leaning forward in his seat he said: 'It would be better if you showed more respect to your superiors, girl. Or do you suppose you are equal to a Tribune?'

Nadira looked down at her mud streaked legs, her torn clothes, wet from the sea and touched her matted hair. She guessed there were scratches and dirty marks upon her face, but she was beyond caring. She shrugged and stared defiantly at the centurion.

'You'll get nothing out of the girl speaking to her like that,' Marcus said thoughtfully. He looked more closely at Nadira.

'Doesn't she remind you of someone we've met before?' he asked.

'Come to think of it,' Julius replied. 'She looks remarkably like the girl who acted as interpreter for Tarkus on our last voyage to these islands.'

Marcus frowned.

'What is she doing here with Higgotty?'

A faint smile appeared on Nadira's face. Marcus glared at the girl, but she stood her ground, staring insolently back. The policeman's name was still difficult for him to get his tongue around, and Marcus supposed the girl to be making fun of his pronunciation of Higgotty's name.

'Is your name, Nadira—daughter of Omega?' Marcus asked haughtily.

'Yes,' she replied rudely.

Marcus nodded satisfied.

'But can we trust her?' Julius wanted to know. 'If we use her as a messenger between ourselves and Tarkus, how do we know if she is part of some trick, which these accursed islanders intend to play upon us?'

Marcus frowned at Julius and shook his head.

'Let me do the questioning.' He turned and faced Nadira.

'Why have you returned with our gift to Tarkus?'

'If I told you the truth you would not believe me,' answered Nadira.

'Try and convince me. You will not find me ungrateful or unfair,' Marcus said.

Nadira tossed her hair back disdainfully. 'Tarkus does not treat your gift with the gratitude he ought to show for

182

something precious. Not only that, he plans to murder you as you all sleep and burn your ship.'

Seeing Marcus's dubious look, Nadira continued.

'I'm serious!' she insisted. 'Tarkus intends to kill you all!'

Marcus and Julius exchanged glances.

'Why have you come to tell us this?' Marcus demanded.

Nadira looked down at her feet, but did not answer. Julius leaned forward and touched his chief on the knee to attract his attention. Seeing that his centurion had important information, Marcus cupped his ear to hear what was being said. When Julius had finished, he nodded slowly.

'I hear you were promised to Tarkus as a bride,' said Marcus sternly. 'I think you are not to be trusted.'

'If you consider my words to be worthless, then put all your trust in Tarkus and then see how much your lives are worth!' Nadira snapped angrily.

'Maybe! Maybe!' Marcus said softly. 'We shall see. But did you have any motives for saving me, my men and the ship? Or,' and he smiled slyly, 'perhaps all your efforts were directed towards helping this unfortunate human?' The Tribune indicated Higgotty. 'I think you love this man, that's why you were willing to risk everything to help him escape. Am I right?'

'You are,' Nadira said shortly. 'But believe me when I say I want to help you as well. As for Tarkus, although you might not believe this, I hate him. I hate him for his cruelty, and would do anything to escape from his clutches.'

'What does she mean?' Marcus asked. 'Why is she so afraid of Tarkus?'

Julius explained. 'This daughter of Omega will die once Tarkus becomes tired of her; all his wives are murdered when he wearies of them.'

'How does he find an excuse to get rid of them? Is there no justice upon this island?' Marcus questioned.

'Tarkus usually has them accused of treason. Usually a trumped-up charge.'

Julius looked at Nadira. 'Is that not so?'

'You must get away from this place; it is not safe,' Nadira insisted. 'Go now, while there is still time.'

Marcus smiled bleakly.

'And play the coward? No. I cannot go yet. besides, some of my men are on shore, bringing back the fresh fruit and dried meat which Tarkus promised us, as part of our agreement.'

Nadira shook her head angrily.

'You are crazy to wait,' she insisted.

A soldier pushed her so that she fell backwards on to the deck. Higgotty leapt forward, but the men guarding him held him back. If Higgotty had broken free, he would have hit the soldier, who had performed such a cowardly act against Nadira. Fortunately, she was not badly hurt, only shaken by the encounter.

'Watch your tongue!' Julius ordered sternly. 'You must learn some respect before you speak to the Tribune.'

She sat up painfully on the deck. 'Brute!' she snapped. 'Is this the way to treat those who come in peace and try to help you?'

Julius turned his back on the girl impatiently.

'How long before your men return?' Nadira asked Marcus.

The Tribune consulted the sun. 'Sometime this evening.'

'You ought to leave as soon as possible,' she insisted.

'And why must I do that?' he smiled.

'There is going to be serious trouble this time, if you don't take action immediately.'

'I will consider your suggestion,' Marcus said. 'And now I must consult my men.'

He signalled to the soldiers guarding Higgotty and Nadira that they were to be taken away. His audience with the prisoners was at an end. Higgotty and the girl were put in the hold of the ship, with the slaves, under the watchful eye of Agricola. They were given fresh clothes to change into, and a meagre ration of water to wash themselves with. Later that day, when the extreme heat had all but stifled them, some food was ungraciously pushed their way. Higgotty couldn't help wondering why such big changes had taken place between the time he had been prisoner on board ship and now. Perhaps it had something to do with the rows which Marcus had been having with Tarkus? As the friction increased between the two leaders, he became more distrustful of everyone, including Higgotty and Nadira.

'How are you feeling?' Higgotty asked Nadira, who was still dabbing at her lip, which was a quite swollen.

'If we don't get away from this place by evening, I don't hold much hope for our chances,' Nadira told Higgotty. She then proceeded to give him a translation of the conversation she had had with Marcus and Julius that morning.

'Let's hope the party bringing provisions for the ship returns soon,' said Higgotty.

'Keep your fingers crossed,' she agreed.

Night fell, but still there was no sign of the soldiers bringing provisions.

'If Tarkus attacks the ship, he will do so tomorrow at first light,' Nadira told Higgotty. 'That way he can surprise the Romans when they are least prepared.'

'In that case, we'd better get some sleep whilst we can,' he suggested.

'Sleep? Is that all you can think of?' Nadira asked indignantly.

'What else can we do but conserve our strength. Besides, it was too hot to sleep earlier,' said Higgotty reasonably. 'Not only that, but they've chained us to the floor.'

Nadira shook her chains irritably. 'I still haven't given up hope that Marcus will suddenly see sense and get us out of this place.' She gave a sudden gasp and abruptly stopped speaking. Higgotty was staring at a man who was making his way slowly their way. Nadira clutched the policeman's arm nervously. Was the man coming to murder them?

'What the devil does he want?' Higgotty muttered. 'And why doesn't Agricola do something?' The slave master was sleeping; his head had fallen on to his chest and he was snorting gently. The mysterious figure continued to inch towards them, until he was so close, Higgotty could have touched him. Nadira opened her mouth, as if to scream, but no sound came, because Higgotty suddenly clapped a hand over her mouth. He had recognised the man.

'Cotta!' he almost shouted. 'Is it really you?'

Cotta nodded violently, delighted that Higgotty recognised him. He began to speak rapidly to Nadira, knowing that she spoke his language. Higgotty listened to Nadira's translation, his mind in a daze. Cotta was the same soldier who had given him that awful spirit to drink, when he had been discovered in the cave beneath the lost city of Tiveria. Once again, Cotta had brought something for them to drink. This time it was in a leather bottle.

Higgotty uncorked the bottle suspiciously, sniffing gingerly.

The soldier laughed wickedly.

'It is all right,' Nadira reassured the policeman. 'Cotta tells me it is some kind of mead; he probably got it in the village. Everyone drinks it.' Higgotty took a swig and then passed the bottle to Nadira.

After they had drunk their fill, the soldier gave them some important information. Marcus had become increasingly nervous since Nadira had issued her warning. Since the soldiers had not returned with provisions for the ship, Marcus was determined to leave the bay at dawn. He had decided to sail to the other side of the island, and there he would teach Tarkus a lesson, if any of his soldiers had been captured or harmed

'Sheer madness!' Nadira muttered. 'That is just what Tarkus wants Marcus to do. He has dug a pit, and Marcus is going to tumble right into it, unless we do something.'

'What can we do?' Higgotty asked helplessly. 'We're prisoners.'

Nadira sighed. Cotta asked a question, and the girl explained the situation to him. The soldier grinned and told her not to worry; then he scuttled back into the shadows.

'What now?' Higgotty wondered.

'Wait and see,' the girl suggested. 'Cotta's obviously got some kind of plan, or he wouldn't look so pleased with himself.'

Unfortunately, whether Cotta had a plan or not was never discovered by Higgotty or Nadira because the next morning Tarkus attacked the *Jupiter*. There was no warning. A flood of arrows whizzed through the air and Marcus's men were forced to dive for cover. Then the policeman and the girl heard a great deal of shouting as a counter-attack was carried out by Marcus. Above them, they could hear the stamping of feet and curses of men as they fought to gain control of the ship. Agricola sat still. He watched over his slaves and the prisoners grimly, wondering if he should send up some of his toughest slaves to help Marcus defend the ship. But could he trust them? To arm a slave was against the rules but to give them nothing to fight with would be futile. In the end, he just sat there waiting, indecision written all over his face.

During the confusion, Cotta made his way into the hold. He called out something urgently to Agricola, and the slave master ran quickly up on deck. Cotta wasted no time, he unlocked the fetters on the girl and Higgotty's legs. He explained that he was doing this to give them a better chance of reaching the comparative safely of the jungle, should the ship be sunk or captured. Nadira shook her head doubtfully at this. She knew that their chances of escaping with their lives would be slim, should Tarkus's men gain the upper hand. Then they crawled up on deck, being very careful to keep out of sight. To their surprise, when they reached the deck, the fighting was almost over. All Tarkus's men had been driven overboard and there was a fierce fight taking place on the shore. Fortunately for Marcus, the men bringing provisions back to the ship had heard fighting going on. They had quickly rushed back to *Jupiter*. By creeping stealthily through the forest, they were able to attack Tarkus's men when they were least prepared. Tarkus was so intent on capturing the Roman ship, that he had neglected to tell his warriors to watch the forest behind them. The Romans seized the advantage and drove their enemies down the beach. So fierce was their attack that many of Tarkus's men threw away their weapons and dived into the sea. By swimming across a narrow channel, they could avoid mass destruction.

Marcus watched the enemy wading out of the sea, climbing a steep bank, before finally running back into the jungle. He knew that it had been more by luck than skilful defence that his men had defeated Tarkus. If Tarkus wanted to, he could muster a greater body of men to attack the ship. Marcus wasted no time in making his preparations to leave the island, as soon as the fresh provisions could be loaded. He ordered Paulinus to take over the navigation of the ship, while he attended to other duties. Cotta took the opportunity of bringing Higgotty and Nadira over to speak to the Tribune.

'So you were right,' Marcus acknowledged.

Nadira bowed her head, knowing that this was the correct thing to do as the Tribune tried to make amends for his mistakes. 'Now that I know you came in good faith to warm me, I will not easily forget those who have proved their loyalty to me. As for your captivity, I can only express my sincere regret for what has taken place.'

'It is to Higgotty you should apologise,' Nadira began.

Marcus spread his hands in a gesture of submission.

'It was a terrible thing for him to be sold into slavery,' she added quietly.

Both Marcus and Julius looked a little uncomfortable at this.

'Politics sometimes override the heart,' Julius explained feebly.

'And money proves stronger than both,' Nadira couldn't help reminding him.

There was an uncomfortable pause, before Marcus laughed and beckoned to a servant, who brought wine and figs for them to eat.

Although both Higgotty and Nadira had been treated shamefully by Marcus and Julius, they had both decided, for the sake of peace, to accept any apology offered. After all, there was little else they could do. To be fair to Marcus and Julius, they did their best to make up for their abominable behaviour. Nothing was too much trouble for their guests, and so the days passed pleasantly enough. They had fair weather and stopped at a couple of friendly islands, where Paulinus could take on fresh water, and put right any deficiencies that had become known following the hasty departure from Tarkus's island. Marcus asked his guests where they wanted to go. The policeman shrugged; he was past caring. Nadira, on the other hand, wanted to get as far away as she could from Tarkus. Her relief at not having to marry Tarkus was plain for everyone to see. She was happy to spend the days chatting to Higgotty. As for the policeman, he could take life easy, following his three weeks as a slave. Eventually, sitting around doing nothing became too much for Nadira. She made herself busy stitching new clothes to replace those which had been ruined during the flight through the jungle. Higgotty was so impressed with the results of her labours, that he begged her to make him a pair of trousers. Nadira agreed to do this.

The day she completed the trousers was a day to be remember by everyone on board *Jupiter*. All the soldiers crowded round, craning over each other's shoulders, so that they could catch a better look at the unfamiliar garments. And when Higgotty first put them on there was a chorus of "oohs" and "aahs". The policeman swaggered up and down the deck; he had never felt at ease wearing a leather kilt. For the first time, since escaping from the desert, he felt properly dressed and more like himself. His trousers had been made from an old piece of sail, and it was difficult to say who was the proudest of the result, Nadira or Higgotty. As for Nadira, she too was dressed in her new finery, having completed a dress for herself in record time. Marcus, to make up for his former boorish behaviour, had supplied her with many fine silks and cloths.

The journey passed pleasantly and several weeks passed since *Jupiter* had Tarkus's island. The weather had been moderately hot, but not unduly unpleasantly and so it was a shock when one day Nadira woke up to find herself shivering. She dressed and went on deck to find out what was happening. There she found Higgotty, Marcus, Julius, Cotta, Paulinus and the others stamping up and down the deck, all wrapped in their military cloaks, shivering and swearing under their breath at the change in the weather.

Seeing her standing there shivering, Marcus came forward and offered Nadira his cloak to wear.

'What has happened?' she wanted to know.

Marcus shook his head in bewilderment.

'No one seems to know.' He leaned forward and whispered in her ear.

'That old fool, Paulinus, thinks he knows where we are, but I don't think he does.'

Nadira couldn't help giggling at this, although she their position was serious.

'Would you show me the chart? Perhaps I might be of help?'

Marcus looked at her doubtfully.

'We have drifted a long way from those islands which paid tribute to Tarkus, your one-time master. I don't think anyone knows where we are. At least, there is nothing marked on the parchment for this part of the ocean.' He showed Nadira the map. His brown face crinkled with a worried frown.

She stared it without comprehension.

'Have you no idea of our whereabouts?' Nadira asked.

'We have tried to take readings from the sun, but our calculations are not making sense; it might as well be the middle of the night for all the use the sun is to us.'

'I wish it was night,' Julius said gloomily, as he made his way over to the Tribune.

'How might the night help us?' Nadira wondered.

'We could find our way by the stars,' Marcus explained.

'I think we should be heading north; the further south we go the colder it gets,' Julius opined.

'Yes, that is strange,' Marcus agreed. 'In our own country, as you probably know, the further north we go, the colder it becomes.' He smiled. 'In my view that is the proper thing to happen. But here -' He shivered. 'I do believe Britannia, which is the furthest north I have been, must hold the record for foul weather, but even that accursed place is not as bad as this place.'

'You are forgetting Iberia, Tribune,' Julius said respectfully. 'There we had snow in the high mountains during the winter campaign.'

Marcus's face took on a faraway look.

'I was forgetting that. But enough of this,' he added briskly.

'What is to be done now?'

'Shall I turn the ship, Tribune?' asked Paulinus.

Marcus nodded. 'I think so. Get the slaves to row us as fast as possible from this terrible place.'

Paulinus leapt to do his bidding, and the ship began to head north.

'We should see an improvement now,' Julius told Higgotty and Nadira. He rubbed his hands together in satisfaction, but he was wrong and conditions did not improve.

A heavy fog settled around the ship, blotting out the sun completely. With whiteness all about them, sending its cold clammy fingers everywhere, Paulinus was forced to rely on a simple lodestone to check the direction in which they were moving. The magnetic properties of the stone helped him to gauge north from south.

'I'm sorry if I got you into this mess,' apologised Higgotty when he saw Nadira. Her arms were wrapped around her body and she was shivering.

193

'At least this is better than being at Tarkus's mercy,' the girl replied, her teeth chattering.

During the afternoon, the fog started to lift. A watery sun began to break through the swirling mists, sending little snatches of brightness flooding out across the water. Then came the sound which was to horrify everyone.

'What is it?' Julius asked in alarm. Marcus signalled to everyone to be silent, whilst he listened. The fog drifted across the sea, eerily spreading out its fingers, like some wispy ghost. Patches of sunlight danced across the water, sending up mysterious reflections into the faces of those who waited.

'There is nothing to see!' exclaimed Paulinus in disgust.

'Tribune! Listen! Over there!' Julius called.

Marcus leaned forward to listen.

Nadira nudged Higgotty and whispered a few words to him. When the girl had finished speaking, Higgotty strained his ears, trying to catch the sound which had first caught Julius's attention. He found himself wishing he could understand more of what was being said, without the girl constantly having to translate every single word which passed between the Romans.

'That's it!' Julius shouted. 'Listen!'

Everyone listened. At first Higgotty could make out nothing, except the gentle lap of the waves against the side of the ship, but even as he listened, the sound of the sea caressing the sides of the vessel appeared to change in pitch. In the distance, like the tolling of a great bell, came a loud roaring sound. Everyone who heard the strange sound guessed that something horrible was about to happen.

'It is the sea-beast!' screamed a voice. Instantly there was a loud wailing from the slaves and some of the soldiers.

'Silence!' snapped the Tribune. He struck the man who had caused such alarm amongst the slaves a heavy blow with his baton.

'Sea-beast!' he snarled. 'You imbecile! There is no sea-beast! Do you hear? There is no such thing. That is the sound of the waves—there is no beast!'

But his words did not check the moaning of the slaves, who began to lapse into their own tongues.

'The sea-beast! Beware the sea-beast!' the slaves moaned.

'Barbarians!' Julius sneered. 'Can you not hear the words of your Tribune? There is no beast! Get back to work!' The angry centurion swung round and faced the cowering soldiers.

'Are you men?' he challenged. He picked up a length of rope and struck the nearest shivering soldier with it.

'On your feet!' he commanded. 'Do you wish that your glorious Tribune, victor in over a score of battles, should consider you a coward?'

'I will fight any man, or army for that matter, single handed,' groaned the man, shaking with terror. 'But I will not fight something I cannot see.'

'Bah!' shouted Julius. He threw the piece of rope at the man.

'If you can hear your enemy, you can fight him, whether you see him or not.'

'It is Neptune—he fishes for us!' one of the soldiers cried.

'Pray to Vesta to save us!' said another.

'You'll need more than Vesta,' sneered Julius. 'Better you should pray to Mars.'

'I have never met such a superstitious lot!' Paulinus declared.

'It is the soft life they have led these last weeks,' Julius said contemptuously. 'Their veins have turned to water; they are little better than the flotsam which floats on the waves.' The tolling of a great bell broke in upon his words. Its deep tones made the planking shake beneath their feet.

When Higgotty felt the deck quiver beneath him and heard the roaring sound become louder, it reminded him of a giant bathtub. It was as if all the water in the ocean had been collected together, before being sucked down into a deep well. He clutched at the girl as the ship began to buck and jump about in the water, as if truly possessed by devils. White flecked water began to dance towards them and the swirling eddies became increasingly frightening as they grew in strength and velocity.

'Pull away from here!' Julius screeched.

The ship immediately became a mass of hasty confusion, with men running about aimlessly, tripping over each other, falling over in their efforts to get the ship away from such a terrible spot.

'What on earth are they so afraid of?' Nadira asked Higgotty.

'I'm not sure,' the policeman replied. 'But if you ask me, it sounds a bit like a whirlpool. Or someplace where the water falls from one level to another.'

'But that is impossible!' Nadira shouted. She turned her face away and turned very pale. Higgotty put his arm around her.

'Are you all right?' he asked gently.

'Yes—it's—it's just that -well, I'm scared!'

'So am I!' Higgotty admitted. Then the ship began to tremble.

'Hold on!' he yelled and grasped her firmly by the arm. The ship gave a sudden lurch, sending several soldiers sprawling.

'Zardaka!' Higgotty yelled.

'What?' shouted Nadira.

'Zardaka! It has to be!' Higgotty roared back.

'I thought it was Neptune,' Nadira said innocently.

Higgotty looked sharply at the girl, half-suspecting that she was making a joke, but he was in error, nothing could be further from her mind. She gave him a sickly smile. The *Jupiter* gave another of its corkscrew tips. Nadira dug her fingers desperately into the splintery wood, hoping she wouldn't be thrown across the deck again. The ship had begun to buck like a horse and there was a grinding crash as the planks strained by a series of shuddering twists and turns. The little vessel began to spin round and round, slowly at first, then with increasing speed. Higgotty felt the ship's timbers begin to loosen beneath his feet. Then water began to gush through gaps in the imperfect planking. Hastily Higgotty picked up a discarded pitcher and began to bail furiously. As fast as he threw the water back where it belonged, more rushed in from a dozen newer leaks in the planking.

'Help me!' he roared desperately. But no one moved. Everyone stared stupidly at Higgotty, except for Nadira, who did her best to help. It was only when the water began to reach the knees of the soldiers that they suddenly woke up to the fact that their vessel was sinking. There was a yell of terror and everyone began to bail furiously. The soldiers used their helmets to throw water overboard. Soon it became a running battle between the bailers and the sea, as an increasing amount of water began to pour through a multitude of leaks. The sea began to win. Eventually, the ship began to list and grew increasingly sluggish in her movements. Soon Higgotty and the girl were up to their waists in water. Then there was a loud crash and a splintering jar as the ship struck something. A huge wave swamped *Jupiter*. Nadira felt herself tugged downwards. She gasped involuntarily as she was forced underwater. Roughly Higgotty hauled her to her feet. Nadira felt her stomach constrict and then she began to vomit water.

'Are you all right?' Higgotty asked.

'Never felt better!' grinned the sick girl.

'That's the spirit!' grinned Higgotty. There was a sharp crack just after he had spoken. They both turned and were just in time to see the mast quiver and then slowly topple overboard with a loud groan of tortured wood.

'We're finished!' gasped Higgotty. Water poured down his face like rain. 'I'm sorry, Nadira, but I did my best.'

'That's all right,' said the girl. 'Thanks for everything.'

She took his arm gratefully.

Higgotty still had time for a few more words of advice.

'Hang on to any piece of wood you can find. That is the only chance you have, especially when we are thrown into the water.'

Nadira screamed as his words were cut off. The ship was lurching downwards, still spinning slowly, as if it were about to enter some giant plug-hole. To the right and left of her, water was rising steeply in a solid wall, green as glass, glistening, reflecting tiny flashes of light, which began to shape themselves into a rainbow. Despite their danger, Nadira was fascinated. The wall of water now rose high above her head, forming a giant tidal wave, which began to curve over the ship. She guessed the wave would suddenly break and smash down upon the ship, crushing it and everyone on board. Somehow the inevitable never happened, because to Nadira's surprise *Jupiter* began to dive, nose first, hurtling through the water like some crazy elevator, whilst the water from the giant tidal wave came thundering down, chasing the ship as it sped downwards into the vortex.

Lord Nimbus

When Stella and the wizard had returned to the spot where they had left Mr Jennings and Dawn, Zardaka clapped his hands loudly. Instantly the two mysteriously shrouded figures appeared.

'Bring food and drink for my guests,' Zardaka commanded.

'Yes, Master.'

'Wait!' The wizard raised his arms.

The figures waited patiently for the next command.

'A change of clothes would be fitting. I do not like to see my guests dressed as they are now.' There was a note of distaste in Zardaka's voice.

'You wish will be obeyed, Master,' promised the figures.

Zardaka turned to his silent guests. With a crooked finger he beckoned to them. He led them to the dining room, a place which was familiar to Stella, but not to Dawn and her father. A long table had been prepared for them, with a white tablecloth, silver cutlery, which gleamed and glistened. Fine long stemmed glasses, filled with wine, stood next to plates of warm appetising food, but when everyone moved forward at the sight, but Zardaka motioned them back. 'I'm sure you would prefer to wash and change first.' He turned to Mr Jennings. 'You will change over there, and the girls can use the other room. Please take off your wet clothes and put on the ones I have provided. Then you can dine. I will join you later.' With that Zardaka strode out of the room. The figures bowed to the guests and then disappeared.

Dumbly, Mr Jennings went to his appointed room, took off his wet things and dressed in the splendid clothes which Zardaka had provided. In the adjoining room, Dawn and Stella were doing the same. There was a small basin, with hot and cold water, so that they could wash themselves, along with a small mirror, which allowed them to tidy their straggling hair.

'My goodness!' Mr Jennings exclaimed when the girls reappeared.

'What a change! I hardly recognise you.'

'Do you like my dress?' Dawn inquired, twirling herself round. She wore a gown of blue, whilst Stella was dressed in red silk. Stella's eyes were sparkling, almost as bright as the gold medallion she wore around her neck. Her honey-coloured hair fell in a shimmering shower down her back. In contrast, Dawn's coal black hair, which was slightly shorter than Stella's, looked equally beautiful against the cool blue of her dress. As for Mr Jennings, he now wore a well-tailored dark navy suit, which suited both his personality and figure.

'Oh, Father!' Dawn exclaimed. 'You look lovely dressed like that.'

'No better than either of you young ladies,' he declared gallantly.

'Come!' he said, giving each an arm. 'Let's go and having dinner.'

'Oh good!' Dawn exclaimed murmured. 'I'm absolutely famished.'

'So am I,' sighed Stella.

'I'm going to taste the food now!' declared Dawn.

'Sensible girl!' exclaimed Mr Jennings pulling out two chairs for the girls. When they were seated, he found himself a place at the head of the table.

Chatting brightly, Dawn and Stella helped each other to large portions of food, whilst Mr Jennings got on with the job of sipping down a hot bowl of soup. Then for a long time there was silence. Eventually, Stella decided she didn't like the wine and would prefer something a little sweeter. She clapped her hands.

'Bring me something decent to drink,' she commanded when one of the shrouded figures appeared.

'Yes, Mistress,' said the figure.

'Stop!' Stella turned to her friend and Mr Jennings. 'Is there anything you want?' she asked. Dawn said she would have whatever her friend wanted, and Mr Jennings said he'd have a cigar. Stella gave the order and within the twinkling of an eye two frothy drinks had arrived for the girls and a cigar for Mr Jennings, together with matches in a silver box.

They were so busy enjoying themselves that they did not hear the wizard return. Sensing that Zardaka had entered the room, their voices died away. Mr Jennings tried to rise from his seat, but Zardaka waved him back.

'I trust you have all enjoyed your meal?' he asked.

Everyone nodded.

'Good!' The wizard cracked his bony fingers together, then he inspected each of his guests narrowly. 'I see the clothes fit; that is good.

'We are grateful, Zardaka, for the…' Stella began, but the wizard interrupted her.

'I will do the talking, if you please,' he said.

Stella shrugged. 'As you wish.'

'There are many things I wish to discuss,' continued the wizard smoothly. 'Such as my plans.'

Mr Jennings shifted uncomfortably in his chair at this.

'Oh don't worry!' Zardaka said, turning upon him. 'I shall also be providing you with a full explanation of my actions. I don't see why I should justify my position,' he added loftily. 'There is nothing you can do to stop me.' He eyed them narrowly, as if watching for dissent. 'You girl!' he said, pointing at Stella. 'You have been very foolish, but you have failed. I hope you now see the error of your ways.' The wizard gave one of his wintry smiles. 'However, I should be grateful to you. You have unwittingly provided me with extra guests. They will make up for those servants you have lost me.'

Stella stared at Zardaka angrily.

'I didn't lose any of your servants; you destroyed Higgotty and that girl, not I.'

Zardaka raised his hand soothingly.

'Of course not. As for destroying them, I think you will find you are mistaken.'

'Then what has happened to Patch?' Stella demanded.

The wizard stroked his beard thoughtfully.

'Patch?'

'Surely you haven't forgotten your little cat burglar already?' Stella asked sarcastically. 'Or is it because he is of no further use, like poor Mr Higgotty?'

'Patch? Oh yes! I remember now,' the wizard mused. 'Something very strange has happened there, as I recall.'

'You mean to say he drowned?' shouted Stella angrily. 'Why...'

'Hush! Please, Stella!' Dawn begged. 'Don't make things worse for any of us.'

Stella drew a long breath. 'All right,' she agreed. 'But what has happened to Patch? I really must know.'

'You would like to meet Patch,' murmured the wizard. 'Well, that I can easily arrange.' He snapped his fingers and the two shrouded servants appeared. 'Bring in the Lord Nimbus,' Zardaka commanded. The figures bowed and disappeared.

'The Lord Nimbus?' Stella asked with bemusement. 'I've never heard of him.'

'No? But soon you shall see your friend,' Zardaka promised Stella.

'Thank goodness for that!'

'Only, I must warn you, you may not recognise him,' Zardaka warned. 'He is very different from the Patch you once knew.'

Stella felt puzzled by Zardaka's mysterious words. She stared helplessly at Dawn and Mr Jennings, wishing she understood more about what was going on. It seemed the more Zardaka explain, the less she understood.

'Here he is,' said Zardaka proudly as a handsome young man stepped into the room.

'Yes, but who is he?' Stella asked in bewilderment. The young man was as dark as a raven, his longish hair curled over the collar of a handsome green jacket. he wore creamy-white knee breeches, silk stockings and a pair of silver buckled shoes. It was just as if someone had stepped out of an eighteenth-century painting. The young man stood gravely in front of the girls and Mr Jennings, with his silk cravat, white gloves and canary yellow waistcoat. He bowed solemnly to each of them in turn.

'This is the Lord Nimbus,' Zardaka informed everyone. 'Stella has met him before on numerous occasions, but unfortunately she does not recognise him now.'

Stella stared at the young man curiously. There was something vaguely familiar about him, but what it was she couldn't decide. Dawn moved slowly forward, so that she could see the young man more clearly. Having bowed to everyone in turn, Lord Nimbus took no notice of the girls, but stared fixedly in front of him, looking at nothing. 'Note the eyes,' invited the wizard.

Both girls did as they were told. Lord Nimbus had the strangest eyes they had ever seen in any young man; they were bright green and feline in character.

'Now look at his fingers,' Zardaka instructed. 'Take off your gloves, you don't need them in here,' he ordered Lord Nimbus. The young man obeyed.

'What long nails he's got!' hissed Dawn in a shocked voice.

'I'd hate to have to shake hands with him. Why doesn't he get them cut,' Stella remarked.

'Never mind that. What does he remind you of?' Dawn asked.

Stella stared hard at the young man, noting the way his hair grew, almost like long strands of fur about his face. She also noted the agile way he stood upon his legs. Then she remembered that Lord Nimbus had made hardly any sound at all when he had walked into the room. 'Why! He's just like a cat!' she said.

'That's exactly what I was thinking!' Dawn agreed excitedly. 'Look at those eyes. Those are cat eyes.'

'And the hands,' Stella observed. She turned towards Zardaka.

'Could Lord Nimbus and Patch be the same person?' she inquired. 'Because this man is half-cat and half-man.'

Zardaka rewarded Stella with a bleak smile and a slight bow.

'Lord Nimbus is my former servant, Patch.'

'Patch!' shrieked Stella in alarm. 'What has Zardaka done to you?' Lord Nimbus took no notice of the girl.

'Calm yourself,' the wizard soothed. 'I have done nothing to him. When he was Patch, he was, shall we say, not exactly himself then. Now he is a little more as he should be.'

'How do you mean?' asked Mr Jennings.

'Well you see, when Patch fell into the fountain with the policeman, Higgotty, he was not his proper shape. Just as the policeman became a snake for a short while, so Lord Nimbus became a cat. My fountain has a curious effect upon things, as your young friend has observed for herself. Therefore, Patch once more became a young man, just as he had been before entering my garden. Unfortunately for him, the spell was not broken completely, hence he appears before you as half-man and half-cat. Given time, no doubt the spell will wear off completely.'

'But why does the young man not speak?' asked Mr Jennings.

Zardaka sighed. 'That too is very curious. In cat shape, as the character Patch, Lord Nimbus had the power of speech. Now he appears to have temporarily lost that

206

ability. It may be, as I have said, the condition will right itself.'

'Can you do anything to help?' Stella asked.

The wizard shook his head.

'I'm afraid it is impossible for me to interfere with someone else's spell.'

'Where did this young man come from originally?' Dawn wanted to know.

'Oh, he's a product of the eighteenth century, that's why I've dressed him as I have. He understands everything I tell him to do, but beyond that, he's less use than he was in cat shape. A pity.' The wizard shook his head regretfully and sighed.

'You mean you can move people through time?' Mr Jennings asked incredulously.

'I can and I have done on many occasions. Ask Stella, if you don't believe me.'

'Is this true?' Mr Jennings asked Stella.

The girl nodded. 'He has shown me the policeman on board a ship with Roman soldiers. His house overlooks just about everything there is to see in our world. He can control the seasons, the weather. He can will the flowers to bloom or wither. When you have seen his garden you will understand.'

Zardaka nodded in a self-satisfied manner.

'Then that could explain those strange goings on in Back Lane,' Mr Jennings said.

'If you like,' the wizard agreed. 'I required people to help me in my initial experiments...'

'Like Stella?' Dawn interrupted.

'Like your friend,' Zardaka agreed. 'Some people have proved unsuitable, but I could not afford to let them return to your world…'

'You killed them?' Dawn asked in a horrified voice.

'No! No! You understand nothing!' exclaimed the wizard angrily.

'Why should I have a need to kill anyone? Look around you; these dancing shapes, flitting above your heads, they are the shapes of those who have offended me. They are not dead. The birds which fly about in the garden, the insects, the flowers and the trees, they are all those who have not carried out my wishes to the letter. They proved unsuccessful to my plan, so I changed them into the shapes that best suited them.'

'How awful!' gasped Dawn with a terrified look upon her face. She did not doubt for one moment that the magician couldn't do what he claimed he could do.

'Oh!' squeaked Stella at Zardaka's terrible admission. 'You really are evil!'

'Am I?' Zardaka made it sound as if Stella had merely rebuked him for putting his shoes on the table, or wiping his knife with a napkin. He did not seem at all bothered by her remarks at all. 'I think I bring order where there is none. I put things right, whilst other construct their lives in utter confusion. Order is the key to progress.'

'But can't you see you have no right to interfere with people in the way you do?' cried Stella desperately. 'Haven't ordinary people got a right to their way of life? Just because you suppose that this is the best way forward for you, it doesn't mean you have unlimited power, or even the right to impose alternative lifestyles on others.'

'Good for you, Stella!' Mr Jennings shouted.

'You really think all of this is important?' Zardaka asked in amazement. 'Soon I shall be the master of the universe and you will all be thanking me for the order I have brought into your lives. Ah! Life then will be indeed something to behold!'

'I think you are crazy,' Stella said candidly.

A faint look of annoyance crossed the wizard's face.

'How can you say such ridiculous things!' he stormed. 'You, a mere child. What do you know of those who command the Grand Oval? I shall be the Master, the one who everyone admires. Everyone will be forced to listen when I speak. They will marvel at my works. I will be Power itself, manifesting myself in the Universe.'

'What good can all this do?' asked Dawn's father. 'And what is this Grand Oval?'

'You ignorant mortal!' said Zardaka. 'Look at your watches! What has happened to them?'

'Mine's stopped!' exclaimed Mr Jennings.

'So has mine, but perhaps I didn't wind it up properly,' Dawn said. Stella didn't bother to look at her watch. She knew it had ceased to work.

'You see?' Zardaka taunted. 'You have no power. You only imagine you have. I have the real power. I can control time.'

'But time is a convention, manmade,' argued Mr Jennings. 'Time only exists for convenience. Just as we use number, one and two and three and so on. It is the same with letters of the alphabet...'

'Then my words mean nothing to you either?' mocked Zardaka. 'You fool! I control your destiny, and the sooner you believe in that, the better! I call the tune now, you must obey. As for you girl,' added the wizard, turning upon

Stella. 'There are to be no more intrigues against me. Understand? You have had your fun.'

'So have you, by the looks of things,' observed Stella.

Back in Higgotty's Time

'This is the strangest country I have ever seen,' remarked Marcus, looking towards White Meadows with troubled eyes. 'Have you any idea where we have sailed to?'

Julius shook his head.

'How about you, shipmaster? You set the course.'

Paulinus scratched his grizzled head with a stupid sort of look upon his face.

'Pah!' exclaimed Marcus in disgust. 'I might have guessed you wouldn't know. Where are my slaves? Come to that, where is the ship? All I can see are my soldiers.'

Both Julius and Paulinus muttered something about sorcery and shuffled their feet uncomfortably.

Nadira gripped Higgotty's arm.

'Do you know where we are?' she inquired.

'Yes. This is my home. Westcutting-on-Sea. I haven't got the faintest idea how we managed to get here though.' The policeman frowned thoughtfully. 'It could have something to do with that rainbow which coiled itself around the ship. That possibly altered the time-scale, so we emerged back into my time.'

'What are you talking about?' asked the girl.

'We're back in the twentieth century. My time. Your mother came from somewhere within this timescale.'

It was small wonder that Marcus found the country strange. The Romans had materialised in White Meadows, just below the reservoir. The railway ran quite close by and a diesel locomotive had just passed, its snub yellow nose preceding a line of light blue coaches. The Roman soldiers stared in disbelief at the procession of carriages. Like film extras in a badly organised film, they huddled beneath the trees at the edge of the meadow, their red cloaks bright against the dullness of the sky. Marcus, splendid as always, in his purple cloak, his breastplate gleaming coldly in the pale watery sunlight, was still muttering something about sorcery to Julius.

'What do you think happened to the slaves and the ship?' Nadira asked.

Higgotty shook his head. 'I don't think any of them drowned; maybe they were returned to their own time-scales.'

'But the Romans haven't.'

'No. But there may be some other reason for that.' Higgotty glanced at his watch. 'Look!' he exclaimed.

'What?'

'My watch! It's working!'

Nadira, who had never seen a watch before, was intrigued and asked Higgotty what it did. Higgotty explained.

'You seemed to be obsessed with time,' Nadira observed. 'When I want to know how much daylight is left, I simply look at the sun.'

'That wouldn't be much good here,' Higgotty observed, pointing at the grey sky above their heads.

'What are you going to do now?'

'Do?' queried Higgotty. 'Why, I'm going down to police headquarters, and then I'm going to give Zardaka a piece of my mind!'

'Dressed like that?'

Higgotty paused. It was as if Nadira had suddenly poured cold water over him. 'You know, you are quite right. I can't go like this. I shall have to get a change of clothes from somewhere.'

'Hold on!' Nadira called out. 'I don't think you're going to have time to do that. Marcus is forming up his men. Do you want me to go over and ask them where they are going?'

'I think you'd better,' said Higgotty with a worried look on his face. 'Heaven knows what will happen if they go tramping around the town dressed like that. Someone might even get killed, with Marcus and his friends in the mood they seem to be in.'

Nadira went over and spoke to the Tribune. Higgotty watched apprehensively as the exchange became rather heated. Eventually, Julius pushed the girl away and the soldiers began to march across the meadow towards the distant houses.

'What did he say?' Higgotty asked.

'Marcus says he will take the town, or perish in the attempt.'

'Oh, no!' groaned the policeman. 'This is all we need!'

'He feels his honour has been compromised.'

'Why?'

'Because Marcus was forced to flee from Tarkus.'

'Oh.'

'Not only that; there is also the loss of the *Jupiter*.
Although Paulinus is in command, it will be Marcus who
will bear the full weight of Rome's shame.'

Higgotty held his head in his hands and groaned.

'He further says,' Nadira continued, 'anyone who
resists his attempt to take over the town will be killed.'

'Did you tell him where he is?'

Nadira nodded grimly.

'Britannia to Marcus is still a Roman Province, so I
couldn't talk any sense into him over that point. Julius was
here once—at Hadrian's Wall!'

'This is all we want!' Higgotty moaned. 'We'd better
follow them and make sure that no harm comes to innocent
people.'

Marcus's men were chanting as they marched across
the meadow. Fortunately, it was early morning and there
was hardly anyone about. Nearly everyone was still in bed.
As they passed through the narrow entrance to the
Meadows, a milkman dropped his crate of milk with a
crash and hid behind his milk cart. Marcus took no notice
of the man, but marched on. The milkman recovered
somewhat, muttering something to himself about crazy
film people as he bent down to inspect about half-a-dozen
broken milk bottles. As they continued to march down the
road, Higgotty had a sudden idea. Why not take Marcus
and his men to Back Lane? Perhaps he could get them into
Zardaka's garden without too much trouble and then it
would be the wizard's problem over what happened next.
Hastily Higgotty told Nadira his plan. Nadira ran down the
line of soldiers and did as she was told. To Higgotty's
relief, Marcus seemed to think finding the most important
citizen in Westcutting-on-Sea a good idea.

214

There was only one casualty on the way, a postman fell off his bicycle as the procession passed him. Higgotty pulled him to his feet.

'Don't say anything to anyone,' he told the man.

'Who are you?' the postman gasped.

'A policeman.'

'Oh yes? And I'm Charlie Chaplin! Do you know something? You're mad! All of you!'

'Perhaps,' smiled Higgotty grimly. A few weeks ago and he might have reacted in much the same way as the postman, but now, he took everything that happened to him for granted.

Before they reached Back Lane the party had to cross the High Street, the same road in which Chris and Paul had tried to catch the shabbily dressed man.

'Higgotty! What are you doing?' shouted a familiar voice.

The constable nearly started out of his skin at the sound of the voice.

'Inspector Gleeson,' he said politely. 'How nice it is to see you, sir.'

'Never mind all that,' said the police inspector grimly. 'What exactly are you up to? And why are you dressed in this ridiculous manner? I thought you were supposed to be on duty.'

'It's rather a long story, sir.'

'Don't be impertinent!' The inspector stood in front of Higgotty quivering with rage.

Marcus asked Nadira something.

'What is he saying? Sounds like a foreign language to me,' said Inspector Gleeson suspiciously.

'It is,' Higgotty said shortly. 'The Tribune was speaking Latin.'

'Don't be funny with me!' snorted Gleeson. 'Latin is a dead language. No one speaks that language nowadays, unless they are locked away in some museum.' He sniggered at his own joke, but before Higgotty could soothe the angry inspector, Julius drew his sword and said something to Higgotty. Inspector Gleeson backed away hastily as the point of a sword was thrust against his neck.

'What—what!' he gurgled, eyes popping out of his head. 'Get this fool away from me!' he spluttered. 'I think he intends to kill me!'

'Put away that sword!' snapped Higgotty.

Nadira said something quickly to Julius, who looked at Marcus. The Tribune nodded, and to Gleeson's obvious relief, the centurion put away his sword.

'You'd better keep your voice down, Inspector Gleeson,' said Higgotty. 'Where these people come from, the sound of an angry voice means trouble; real trouble!'

Gleeson backed away to safe distance gibbering with rage.

'You'll be hearing more about this, PC Higgotty!' he stuttered. 'And let me tell you, no one threatens me in broad daylight with a sword, even if he is a cheap actor!'

Higgotty sighed. 'I'm telling you the truth. Stick around and find out for yourself.'

'I think I have already found out the truth,' said Gleeson grimly. He mopped his face with a very large, very white handkerchief. 'I'm going back for reinforcements,' he added. 'And I shall want a full explanation from you when I get back!' The Inspector turned towards the kerb, where a patrol car was standing.

216

'I'm calling for reinforcements. That'll show you lot I mean business.'

'Oh, dear!' groaned Higgotty. 'I'm really in for it now!'

'Is he your chief?' asked Nadira.

'Sort of. We'd better get a move on.'

'Why?'

'Because Gleeson is about to radio HQ.'

Nadira nodded understandingly, and said something to Marcus. The Romans resumed their march, leaving Gleeson babbling into his microphone, desperately trying to explain the situation to Headquarters. Whilst Gleeson was still on the radio, Higgotty took Marcus and the soldiers to Back Lane.

'Bother!' exclaimed Higgotty.

'What is wrong?' asked Nadira.

'I don't seem to be able to find the green door in the wall.'

'Green door? What door is that?'

'I can't explain now, it would take too long, but it is the way into Zardaka's place.'

'Then you'd had better hurry up and find this door, before your boss gets back,' suggested Nadira. 'Do you think we could get the men over the wall, before there's trouble?'

Higgotty glanced at the glass topped wall critically. 'It's worth a try. Romans are renowned for their ingenuity, aren't they? Now, let's see if they can climb walls.'

One of the soldiers produced a rope ladder, after Nadira had explained the situation to Marcus. As Gleeson and his men arrived, the ladder was being thrown up the wall, so that its pointed hooks, which weighted one end of

217

the ladder, gripped the wall firmly. 'Stop exactly where you are!' bellowed Inspector Gleeson, as the Romans prepared to launch themselves over the wall.

'Don't be a fool, Gleeson!' Higgotty snapped. 'You are meddling in something you don't understand.'

'Fool? How dare you!' The Inspector blinked in surprise. Never once, during the whole of his long career in the police force, had anyone dared to speak to him as Higgotty had dared. 'I think you are forgetting yourself, PC Higgotty!' Gleeson said sharply. 'Move out of the way, or I'll have you all arrested.'

'On what charge?' Higgotty challenged, playing for time, seeing that the Romans had secured their ladder and that one of the soldiers was already in the process of scaling the wall.

'Obstruction, aiding and abetting criminals, consorting with madmen, endangering the peace of the town and kidnapping,' Gleeson replied smoothly.

'Kidnapping! Just who have I kidnapped?' sneered Higgotty.

'Stella Holmes,' the inspector returned.

Higgotty's mouth opened wide in astonishment.

'What! Have you gone completely insane, Inspector?'

'No—but I think you have. Arrest that man, sergeant!'

'Believe whatever you like!' Higgotty shouted, fending off the arm that tried to grasp his. 'We are going over the wall whether…'

The rest of his words were cut off by the sound of a loud explosion, which destroyed part of the wall in a sudden burst of orange flame. The explosion was followed by a cloud of yellow dust which made everyone cough and splutter. In the confusion, Higgotty, Nadira and Marcus and the Romans managed to get away.

Pirates in My Wardrobe

'Is something wrong?' Mr Jennings inquired.

'I'm not sure,' Stella replied.

'But I thought when you described your room to me, it had things scattered around it,' Dawn reminded her friend.

'Not quite like this,' Stella murmured. 'It looks as if someone has been messing around. I wonder who it could have been?'

Her words caused a chill to settle over the room. Mr Jennings moved uneasily over to the window and took a furtive glance outside. He could see nothing; the sky was black and overcast. Then, as he turned to face them, a howl sounded.

'What on earth was that?' Mr Jennings gulped.

The eerie sound of a wolf howling in the forest could clearly be distinguished.

'That is a wolf!' Dawn declared. 'I've heard them howl in nature films.'

'What do you expect?' Stella asked indifferently. 'This part of the house overlooks a Canadian forest.'

'A what?' gasped Dawn.

Stella shrugged. 'It's just the way I described it to you. I knew you didn't really believe me, when I told you Zardaka's house overlooks the world. You see, different

220

windows look out across different countries. This particular window overlooks Canada.'

'What a good way of learning geography, without having to look at boring maps,' Dawn sighed.

'The time factor!' exclaimed Mr Jennings. 'So Zardaka really is able to use time to suit his own designs.'

'That is what he said at dinner,' his daughter reminded him.

Mr Jennings yawned. He suddenly felt tired. It had been a long day. His yawning started the girls yawning as well.

'Oh my!' he exclaimed. 'I do feel sleepy! How do you two feel?'

'I wouldn't mind going to sleep right now,' Stella confessed.

Mr Jennings looked about him.

'You could share this room,' he suggested. 'I can sleep on the couch in the other room. The bed here is large enough for you both to share.' Mr Jennings shook his watch impatiently. It had stopped the moment he had entered Zardaka's world.

'Good night!' he said and closed the door behind him. The girls climbed on top of Stella's bed, without undressing, and within a few minutes were both sound asleep.

As for Mr Jennings, it seemed as if he had only just closed his eyes before he was awake again. Something, or someone, had caused him to jerk wide-awake. He could hear someone creeping around the couch, issuing creepy whispering sounds. He felt his flesh crawl. He wondered if burglars had broken into the house, because there were plenty of nice things to steal. He strained his ears, but he couldn't make out what the noise was.

'Who's there?' Mr Jennings knew he had made a terrible mistake when he opened his mouth. He felt a hand seize him and drag him off the couch. Startled, Mr Jennings lashed out with his fists. There was a grunt of pain and the hand relaxed its grip and Mr Jennings could wriggle free and hide beneath the couch.

'Mr Jennings! Mr Jennings!' screamed Stella. 'There are soldiers everywhere!'

Dawn's father heard the girls screaming and hastily made his way towards them, dodging beneath the legs of the struggling men, who had for no logical reason started to fight one another. Where these armed men had appeared from, he could not tell, but there they were, struggling and grappling with each other, knocking glasses and china ornaments on to the floor, grinding precious bits of porcelain into the expensive carpet, as they fought for control of the room.

'What are we going to do?' Dawn screamed. She watched in horror as a fierce warrior snatched a picture from the wall and smashed it over his adversary's head.

'Let's get out of here!' Mr Jennings shouted.

'Which way?' chorused the girls.

'Out of the window.'

'What?' queried Stella.

'Don't argue!' snapped Mr Jennings. 'Make a run for it.'

Dawn and Stella didn't hesitate. A nasty looking pirate was racing towards them.

Mr Jennings was only able to dodge the spear the man threw by good fortune, giving a gasp of astonishment as it flew over his head and buried its point in a rather fine ornamental table, breaking off one of its legs. Whilst Mr Jennings held his ground, the girls fled screaming towards the window. Awaiting his chance, he waited until the man came nearer and then whacked the pirate across the shins with a brass curtain rod, which he had found lying on the girls' bed. As the man fell on the floor, roaring with rage, another pirate jumped on top of him and they began to swap punches. To the pirates, it was all a game. They didn't mind who they fought, just so long as they could engage in their favourite sport. Mr Jennings didn't waste any time watching the two struggling men, he hurried to the window to assist the girls.

'Come on! Let's go!' he commanded.

Ignoring Stella's protests over the dangers of going through the window, Mr Jennings took hold of both Stella and Dawn and bundled them out of the window, so that they were standing on a narrow ledge. As Mr Jennings made his escape, he felt his legs grasped by one of the pirate. He kicked out wildly and squeezed the rest of his body through the window. As he inched his way towards the girls, a fierce face appeared at the window, wielding a huge cutlass. Dawn screamed as the pirate leaned forward and hacked the curtains to pieces in his efforts to reach her father. Balancing themselves precariously on the ledge, the three fugitives backed away in alarm as the pirate's terrible sword swept past their faces. Stella felt as if she were in the grip of some nightmare as the pirate's red eyes glittered evilly. So long as she lived, she would never forget that terrible face, with the long livid scar running down the whole of the left side of the pirate's face. The man shouted something horrible at them and redoubled his efforts to wound them with his sword.

'I can't stand much more of this!' Dawn moaned. 'I'm think I'm going to either be sick or faint.'

'Hold on to my hand,' begged Stella. 'Don't give up now.'

The pirate began to yell awful sounding words at them, his red eyes glittering madly.

'Oh!' gasped Dawn and for an awful moment it looked as if she would fall. Luckily for everyone, it wasn't Dawn who fell from the ledge, but the pirate. One moment he was there, glowering, cursing, shaking his cutlass, hacking great notches out of the brickwork in his efforts to reach them, and then the next moment he had gone. Had he overbalanced? Or had he been pushed? They heard a long wailing scream, which was cut short by a huge crash as the pirate hit the ground.

'Do you think he's badly hurt?' asked Dawn, her eyes round with fear.

'I certainly hope so!' exclaimed Mr Jennings unsympathetically. 'It was either him or us. He wouldn't have given us a sporting chance, so why should we care about him?'

'What are we to do now?' Dawn asked. 'Do we go back into the room?'

'No—no! we can't risk going back,' Mr Jennings said decisively. 'There could be more pirates waiting for us.'

'Where on earth did they all come from?' Dawn wanted to know.

Stella gave a gasp. 'Of course!' she exclaimed. 'They are the ornaments come back to life.' When Mr Jennings looked puzzled, Stella tried to explain further. 'But don't you see? Those ornaments which were scattered around the house have regained their proper shape. I expect they were lying there under some enchantment.'

'How do you mean?' Dawn asked.

'I mean the spell which Zardaka has cast upon them has been broken,' Stella said. 'Unfortunately, they remained in the wrong time zone. Don't you see that?'

'I think so,' Mr Jennings said doubtfully.

'What do we do now?' Dawn inquired. 'I'm getting a little cold up here. I'm also still frightened of falling.'

'We could creep along the ledge and see if we can get in through another window,' suggested Mr Jennings.

'That would be better than sitting out all night perched on this ledge,' agreed Stella.

They crept back along the ledge for what seemed a long time. No one wanted to talk and the dark brooding intensity of the unseen forest, somewhere out the distance, made them very cautious of where they put their feet. One slip and they would join the dead pirate. Even if they survived the fall, there were wolves in the forest which would complete the job which the pirates had left unfinished. Suddenly they came across a lighted window. Mr Jennings inched himself upwards.

'What can you see?' Dawn demanded impatiently.

'Not much—wait a bit!' came the reply. Mr Jennings was by now standing on his toes.

'I think I can see that policeman friend of yours and two boys.'

'Chris and Paul!' Stella squeaked with delight. She felt quite breathless, so great was the shock of finding Mr Higgotty again and the boys.

'I can't be certain,' said Mr Jennings. 'The policeman is not in uniform, but he looks very familiar to me. As for the boys, you'll have to judge for yourself.'

Mr Jennings, with assistance from his daughter, hoisted Stella up so she could look. Breathing heavily with excitement, Stella peered through a gap in the curtains; she could see an unfamiliar young woman, several years older than herself, dressed in armour and with. several soldiers looking exactly like the ones Zardaka had shown her in his strange vessel of water. Then she gave a cry of astonishment.

'Here! Steady on!' Mr Jennings warned as the girl's foot accidentally kicked him.

'Sorry!' Stella apologised. 'Did I hurt you?'

'The heel of your shoe has made a hole in my ear, but why should I bother about that?'

'Never mind about that!' Dawn said excitedly. 'Did you see them?'

'Yes! They are all there! Oh, it will lovely to say 'hello' to everyone again.'

'Well, knock on the window and ask them to let us in,' grumbled Mr Jennings. 'I shall freeze to death out here in a minute.'

Stella did as she was told.

'Where on earth have you been?' Higgotty asked crossly.

'That's just what I was going to ask you!' Stella countered cheekily.

Mr Jennings and Dawn stood blinding in the brightly lit room, staring at the grim-faced soldiers. Although the Romans looked on suspiciously, they stayed apart from Mr Jennings and the girls.

'The last time I saw you,' said Stella addressing Chris and Paul. 'You were in a terrible shipwreck. I thought you were both dead.'

'No—we were stuck on the island with hardly anything to eat for ages,' said Paul.

'Then a rainbow suddenly appeared over the island...' interrupted Chris.

'And took us back to the house,' finished Paul.

'It only happened about an hour ago,' added Chris.

'I found they wandering around the house, when I came in with Marcus and his men,' Higgotty explained.

'It's a long story,' said Paul.

'And we don't have time for stories now,' Higgotty interrupted firmly.

'But how did you get away?' asked Stella.

'Oh, that's another long story.' Higgotty frowned impatiently. 'I'll tell you the rest later.'

'Who's the very distinguished looking man?' inquired Mr Jennings.

'That is Marcus. He is a Roman Tribune.'

'And look over there!' Dawn exclaimed.

'Oh, you've found Lord Nimbus!' Stella said excitedly. 'You know who he is?'

Higgotty shook his head. 'No I don't. Julius found him wandering around in what looked like a laboratory.'

'Lord Nimbus is Patch!' Stella said triumphantly.

'We can't believe it!' chorused the boys.

'See! He is still is under a spell. That's why he appears as half-man and half-cat,' Dawn added.

The two girls and boys began to chat excitedly.

'Sorry to break up your reunion party,' Higgotty said firmly, 'but what we must do now is stop Zardaka. There

227

will be plenty of time for swapping stories once that task is accomplished. All the soldiers with me are Romans from the ship I was wrecked in. This young lady is Nadira, and I literally owe my life to her.' Higgotty paused so that Stella could greet Nadira, the young woman she had seen the policeman with on board the ship.

'It is pointless me telling you who my Roman friends are,' said Higgotty. 'They only speak Latin. Nadira is the only one here who can speak their language. They cannot speak our language because we exist outside their time zone, but further explanations will have to wait. Now, follow me.'

Higgotty stopped at the bottom of the stairs. He sensed that something was wrong. Yellow smoke coiled itself about his feet.

'What do you think is going on?' asked Stella.

'I think either Zardaka's house is on fire,' the policeman replied. 'Or this smoke could be a sign of his ebbing powers.'

'I agree,' said Mr Jennings. 'Something has gone drastically wrong with Zardaka's world.'

'What on earth is that noise?' inquired Dawn.

Everyone paused to listen.

'It sounds like a great bell,' Nadira observed.

'It is,' said Higgotty.

'And there is a ticking noise, it sounds like a great clock,' Stella said.

'Are we going down further?' Nadira asked. 'It is very dark over there.'

'I'm not sure,' Higgotty said uncertainly.

Marcus called out a warning and everyone came to an abrupt halt.

There was a scraping of steel from somewhere directly in front of them. Stella screamed. The soldier immediately formed themselves into a semi-circle, under Marcus's orders to protect Higgotty and his companions. In the torch light, Dawn and Stella could see the vicious looking pirates ready and waiting to attack anyone who opposed the wizard. Chris and Paul winced, whilst the girls hid their faces from the awful sight. Then, there was a well-remembered low pitched laugh, causing Stella's blood to turn to ice. She caught Higgotty by the arm.

'It's Zardaka!' she warned. 'Do be careful!'

Higgotty didn't say anything, but he did pat her hand reassuringly.

'Welcome!' said the voice. Chris and Paul started. It was just as if they were waiting beside the fountain again. Dawn and Mr Jennings felt the same as the boys, only Stella and Higgotty appeared calm and collected.

'Enjoy your little shipwreck?' Zardaka asked Chris and Paul.

'Not much,' muttered Paul.

'We could have been drowned for all you cared,' growled Chris.

'Ah! But I expect you enjoyed your dunking in the sea,' taunted the wizard.

'Just much as the girls liked your snowstorm,' Higgotty replied.

'Yes, that was rather pretty, wasn't it? And what about your imprisonment? Although it seems that you have made friends with your former captors.'

'Yes, and you might live to regret that,' said Higgotty. 'In any case, you might as well admit, Zardaka, I think the members of the Grand Oval have defeated you, unless I'm much mistaken.'

Zardaka frowned. 'How do you know that?'

'We found Patch, or Lord Nimbus, if you prefer, in your laboratory, he was doing something to the clock.'

'So! A simple cat, which I once trusted, has unleashed time!' Zardaka said viciously. 'I'll get even with you all later!'

'Stop bluffing!' snapped Higgotty. 'You've lost. Let us pass. No doubt the members of the Grand Oval will soon be here to pick you up. I suggest you let us go.'

'Indeed? Is that all?' sneered the wizard.

There was a sudden crash, as if part of the wizard's house had fallen in.

'That is your answer, Zardaka. That was the sound of your world breaking up,' Higgotty said contemptuously. 'Minute by minute your power is dissolving and soon there will be nothing left, except one or two pieces, which you might like to pick up and put in your pockets, just to remind you of what you once possessed.'

'Very funny!' Zardaka said viciously.

'So, will you let us pass?'

'No!' thundered Zardaka. 'I'm going to destroy you all! You think you can play games with me and get away it? No! By thunder I'll see you all in hell before I lose all that is precious to me.' He shouted an order and the pirates rushed forward. Even as Zardaka spoke Higgotty and Stella were pulled back by the Roman soldiers, who formed a wall with their shields. Desperately the evil forces of Zardaka tried to break through the ring of soldiers, to get at Higgotty and his friends, but each time they charged, a few more of their number lay defeated on the floor. Soon there were none, and Zardaka stood alone.

'Give up, Zardaka!' ordered Higgotty. 'We will show mercy.'

'No! I'd rather die first!' shouted the wizard.

He turned to flee, but Lord Nimbus was on him in a trice, spitting and scratching as he launched a terrible attack upon his former master. Zardaka managed to snatch a sword from the floor just in time to defend himself with. Round and round they went, exchanging blows with each other. They were evenly matched and as the fight progressed, even Marcus and his men were impressed with the bravery of the wizard. They would have liked to have intervened, but it was not in the Roman nature to interfere in such a personal battle. In any case, if they had tried to stab Zardaka, the result might have been injuring Lord Nimbus instead. So they just stood and waited for an opportunity to take on the wizard themselves, should he win the fight. It was Lord Nimbus who suddenly decided to end the fight finally. He made a tremendous leap over the head of his adversary, intending to stab the wizard in the back. Immediately Zardaka seized his chance. He slashed the cat-man from chin to belly. Lord Nimbus gave a terrible shriek of agony and fell bleeding on the floor. Marcus yelled to his men to kill the wizard, but they were too late. Zardaka with his considerable strength thrust the soldiers back with his bare hands, shoving them so hard that they fell over like ninepins. Then he made his escape.

'Let him go!' shouted Higgotty. 'It doesn't matter anymore. We've destroyed his world.' But Stella threw herself on her knees sobbing at the side of Lord Nimbus.

'Oh, Patch!' she cried. 'Has Zardaka killed you? Oh, please don't die.' Dawn and the boys also crowded round the stricken cat-man. To everyone's amazement, despite his deep wounds, Lord Nimbus continued to breathe. Even as they looked, the bleeding stopped. Dawn peered at the motionless figure curiously.

'Look!' she cried. 'Something wonderful is happening. I do believe!'

Higgotty pushed forward. He knelt beside Lord Nimbus.

'Can you see?' Dawn inquired.

'His hands look normal,' Stella said in a puzzled voice.

'Yes,' agreed Higgotty. 'And look at his face; he has lost that cat-like look. Even the fur round his face has changed.'

Lord Nimbus opened his eyes. Stella gasped. The young man's face had been transformed. His eyes were no longer green—they were blue! Even his hair looked normal, though long by modern standards.

'Patch!' Stella cried. 'Are you all right?'

The young man sat up.

'Who are you?' he asked. 'Why do you keep addressing me as Patch? And where is that evil old man who was attacking me? Why are all these people staring at me?'

He sounded so haughty and puzzled, Chris and Paul couldn't help laughing. Lord Nimbus looked at them angrily. 'How dare you laugh at me!' he snapped. 'Do you not know what I am?'

'You are quite safe now,' Dawn assured him.

'But what has happened? Why am I here?' demanded Lord Nimbus.

'Oh dear!' Stella wailed. 'He doesn't know us.'

'You are quite safe with us,' Dawn tried to reassure Lord Nimbus. 'You have suffered a very great shock, that is all. Just lie there and rest awhile.'

Lord Nimbus ignored her and insisted on rising to his feet. As he stood up, a curious thing happened as something fell away from his body.

'What's that?' Stella asked in panic.

'It is his cat-skin,' said Higgotty.

'How horrid!' shuddered Dawn.

'Look! It is peeling away from his body!' shouted Chris.

Everyone crowded round to look.

'Another miracle!' marvelled Higgotty.

There was a loud rumble and a crash from somewhere nearby.

'I think we'd better be getting out of this house,' Nadira suggested nervously. 'It sounds as if it were about to fall down.'

No one wasted any time in getting out of the house. Just as the last soldier rushed past the two stone lions which guarded the entrance to the house, there was a terrible explosion. 'Get away from the house!' yelled Higgotty. 'I think something terrible is about to happen!'

At the End of the Rainbow

From a safe distance, they watched as with a loud groan the wizard's house began to settle into its foundations. A fire appeared to be spreading throughout the house, so that the tall pointed windows glowed with strange coloured flames. The walls began to bulge, and then without any further warning the house suddenly crumpled like a piece of burning paper and turned into nothing!

'Look at the trees!' exclaimed Stella.

Before their very eyes, the trees began to wither. The birds that were left in the garden began to hack and peck the fruit to pieces. In a frenzy of unpredictable greed, they even gobbled up the tattered leaves, until nothing remained. Then they flew away. 'Let's get over to the fountain,' suggested Higgotty. 'That is where everything began and that is where I think the final spell will end.'

Under Higgotty's direction, the Romans lined up beside the fountain. Marcus, grave and rather pale underneath his tan, clasped the policeman's arm for the last time. The two men said nothing, but Higgotty could read the professional admiration for him in the Tribune's face. Julius also clasped the policeman by the arm, whilst the rest of the Romans contented themselves with smart salutes, made with the right hand held across the breast. This was followed with shouts of homage, which Nadira later translated. Then, one by one, the men jumped into the fountain, never flinching, their trust placed entirely in Higgotty, who had guided them through this strange land. When the last Roman had splashed into the fountain, Stella asked Higgotty a question.

'Do you really think Marcus and his men will be returned to their own time?'

'Yes. Don't you? Besides, I can't see what else we could have done.'

'I think that fountain is the only true way out of the garden,' Chris said. 'After all, when Paul and I tried the forest we could not break free of Zardaka.'

'We simply wasted a great deal of time on some tiny island, till it suited Zardaka's purpose to bring us back. Then we met you all,' Paul agreed.

Dawn was still craning her head over the bowl of the fountain, to see what would happen to Marcus and his men. It was somewhat disappointing; only a trail of bubbles marked the soldiers passage, nothing more.

'So, what happens next?' Stella wondered.

'I expect you will find out soon enough,' said a well-remembered voice. Stella swung round in alarm.

'You!' she gasped.

Zardaka bowed his head and smiled.

'No soldiers to help you all out this time,' he observed.

'You are under arrest, Zardaka!' snapped Higgotty.

'Oh?' sneered the wizard. 'And how do you propose to arrest me? Remember, although my powers are somewhat reduced of late, I am still ten times stronger than you. So what do you propose to do about arresting me, eh?'

'He's quite right, you know,' Chris whispered to the policeman

'There is another thing you are all forgetting,' Zardaka added.

'Tell us then,' Higgotty growled.

'It is simply this,' Zardaka said slowly. He was enjoying making everyone uncomfortable. 'You haven't gotten away from this place yet, have you?'

Higgotty stared at Zardaka, dislike for the wizard plainly written all over his face.

'In fact,' continued Zardaka, who was rapidly beginning to regain his old form. 'You have no chance of getting away from this place without my help.'

'Oh, really?' Higgotty inquired sarcastically. 'What gave you that idea. Take hold of him Lord Nimbus!'

'Don't you dare touch me!' screeched Zardaka.

'Stay where you are!' commanded a voice.

Everyone stood still, hardly daring to breathe. The voice had that sort of authority.

'Zardaka is my prisoner,' said the voice.

'And who are you?' Stella asked boldly.

'You will find you know me well enough,' the voice replied.

'That voice,' said Mr Jennings. 'It appears to be coming from out of the fountain. What on earth is going on?'

Mr Jennings question was answered almost immediately by the appearance of a mysterious blue bird. In fact, it was the same bird which Chris and Paul had met in the forest. The bird flew over the heads of everyone, causing the spray from the fountain to turn into a series of coloured rainbows. Then the bird alighted on the grass before the assembly, puffed out its breast and began to sing with such a melting flood of golden notes that everyone, except for Zardaka, who remained stony faced throughout, found themselves transfixed by a variety of emotions. The bird's song ended abruptly and it began to hop round and round the fountain. Each movement brought the bird nearer and nearer to Lord Nimbus.

'Oh dear!' gasped Stella. 'I do hope Lord Nimbus doesn't forget himself!'

Her fears were quite unnecessary There was a violent flash of light, followed by a loud explosion. When their eyes could focus again, the bird had gone and in its place stood a lovely lady, dressed in a silken gown of blue. She was no ordinary lady though; her skin shone with a silvery kind of light. Even her hair, so long and flowing, shimmered, as if it were fashioned out of some rich metal, which had then been teased into delicate strands. Around her neck she wore a strange device, which looked rather like a medallion of some kind. This medallion glittered with such blinding light that everyone was forced to squint or turn their heads away. It was almost as if the lady was wearing a miniature sun about her throat. With a floating kind of movement, the lady glided towards the wizard.

'Ah, Zardaka!' she exclaimed. 'It's been such a long time since we last met. But you don't seem very pleased to see me?'

'What do you want of me, Mistress of the Stars?' asked the magician in a shaky sort of voice.

'It is not what I want, it is what the Grand Oval require. They have sent me to tell you that they have relieved you of your powers. I think you know what that means?'

'What?' Zardaka's mouth dropped open. 'But they can't!'

237

'Can't they?' asked the blue gowned lady sternly. 'I am afraid you are mistaken, they just have!' Zardaka stared helplessly at her. 'Try your powers, if you don't believe me,' the Mistress of the Stars invited. A glimmer of hope appeared on the wizard's face. He raised his left hand and pointed it at the blue gowned lady. Breathlessly everyone watched to see what would happen. Zardaka muttered a string of words in a strange language, but nothing happened. The Mistress of the Stars smiled.

'You see, Zardaka, your powers have gone and now you are as mortal as these good people standing beside you.'

'But I don't want to be mortal!' Zardaka howled. 'I want my powers back!'

'You've played with fire once too often, Zardaka. Now you are going to find out what it is like to get burned. Little boys who play with matches deserve to get hurt, don't they?' Her question was directed at Stella, Dawn, Chris and Paul. The four children nodded solemnly. 'You see, these boys and girls understand, even if you don't, Zardaka. It is no good you squealing this time, because the Grand Oval have instructed me to put an end to your wicked ways.'

'Mercy!' cried the wizard in such a piteous voice that even Stella felt a little sorry for him. The Mistress of the Stars felt no such pity for him though, and she told the wizard so. 'Mercy? Do I hear you cry for mercy? Why should I show you mercy when I have seen the evil things you do? No—I shall show you no mercy.'

'Please—I can make amends'

'For Lord Nimbus? For Stella's imprisonment? For nearly drowning Mr Higgotty and his companions? For terrifying two boys with that awful storm? Have you already forgotten that business at the supermarket? The list goes on and on, doesn't it? I haven't forgotten the business of turning Mr Higgotty into a snake. That was hardly the behaviour of a responsible wizard, was it? Only the bravery of this young lady here saved Mr Higgotty from a terrible life of misery.' Nadira blushed as the Mistress of the Stars pointed her out to the gathering. 'So you see,' said the Lady triumphantly. 'It is a little too late for making amends for your abominable behaviour.'

'What do you want of me?' demanded Zardaka.

'You know what you have to do.'

When Zardaka hesitated the Mistress of the Stars tapped her foot impatiently. Slowly, the wizard moved towards the fountain. 'Up with you!' ordered the Lady. Reluctantly Zardaka climbed on to the rim of the crown shaped fountain. The stone dolphins began to gush water through their mouths, causing the spray to rise higher than Chris or Paul remembered it rising on any previous occasion. Then a rainbow began to appear. It was a most beautiful sight, but the Mistress of the Stars took no notice of it. 'Get up on the ledge!' she rasped. She raised her left arm and great blue streamer of fire flew from her fingers, like some mighty lightning bolt. The flash of light struck Zardaka a terrible blow in the breast. He gave a terrible shriek, which was followed by a deafening crash, like thunder. To everyone's amazement, the wizard suddenly burst into a ball of flame and fell hissing into the fountain. Another explosion followed when the fireball hit the water. Great gouts of water flew steaming into the air.

'Get back! Get back!' shouted Higgotty.

At last the steam cleared away, they could see the water.

'There isn't anything there,' said Paul disappointed.

'What did you expect?' asked the Lady in an amused voice.

'Have you done something very terrible to Zardaka?' Stella asked nervously.

The Mistress of the Stars took her by the arm.

'Don't worry,' she reassured the girl. 'I have prepared a special place for Zardaka, a place where he cannot repeat his past wickedness. He is not really dead. He only appears that way to your world.' As Stella looked into the bright sapphire eyes and somehow she felt comforted. The blue gowned lady was the most beautiful person she had ever known; she felt quite sure that the Mistress of the Stars knew what was best. 'Aren't you going to jump into the fountain?' Higgotty asked Nadira.

'Whatever for?' inquired the girl.

'It may be your only chance of returning to your own time,' Higgotty explained.

'But I want to stay here with you,' Nadira replied. 'You know I have no life back in that village. Please let me stay here with you.'

Higgotty smiled. 'Whatever you say,' he agreed.

Then he turned to the others.

'Come along, we have a great of business to get sorted out. I doubt whether Inspector Gleeson will believe anything I have to say, but at least I have you all as witnesses.'

'I certainly hope we get off that shoplifting charge,' Chris murmured to Paul.

They all began to make their way out of Zardaka's garden.

'Whatever happened to the Mistress of the Stars?' Dawn suddenly asked.

'Oh, she's gone without saying good-bye,' Stella said in a disappointed voice.

'More likely she had to go, because someone should look after that dreadful Zardaka,' Dawn suggested.

'And where is Lord Nimbus?' asked Chris.

'Oh, has he also gone?' cried Stella. 'I did so want to say goodbye to him.'

'Come on! Let's get home!' said Mr Jennings and he linked arms with the girls.

'Come along! Our work is done here.'

Nadira and Mr Higgotty walked in front, with Chris and Paul following behind them, then came Mr Jennings with Dawn and Stella, who were chattering like two magpies.

'I expect they'll be all right,' muttered Paul to Chris. 'But do you think that store manager will believe us, when Mr Higgotty gets us back to the station?'

'We have enough witnesses on our side this time,' Chris replied.

'Yes, you and that Belinda!' teased Paul.

'Oh, shut up!'

The End